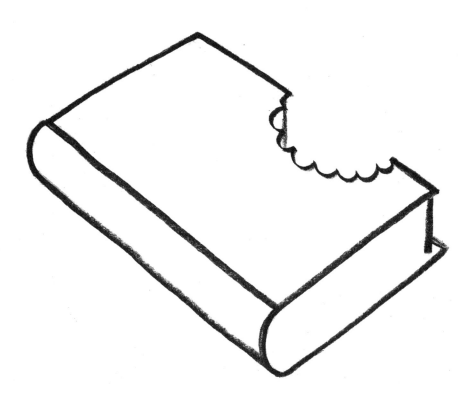

New York City, Winter 2001–2002
Number Fourteen

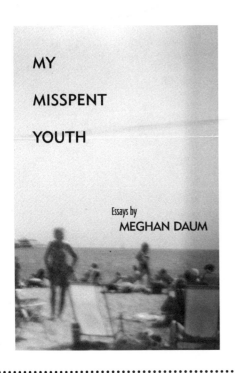
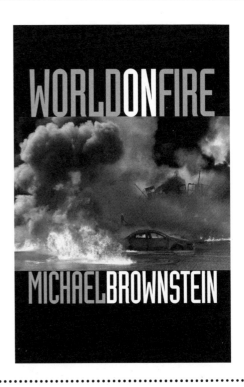

123 watts

Piot Brehmer

Davide Cantoni

Marti Cormand

Mark Ferguson

Teo Gonzalez

Gary Gissler

Robert Jack

Marco Maggi

Stefana McClure

Jean Shin

Julianne Swartz

123 Watts Street
New York, NY 10013

tel: 212.219.1482
fax: 212.274.1726

www.123watts.com
gallery@123watts.com

OPEN CITY

LINCOLN PLAZA CINEMAS

Six Screens

63RD STREET & BROADWAY
OPPOSITE LINCOLN CENTER
212-757-2280

The Prognosis:

"The news was bad. I was dying of something nobody had ever died of before. I was dying of something absolutely, fantastically new."

The Subject Steve

A NOVEL

Sam Lipsyte

Chuck Palahniuk prescribes bed rest:

"I laughed out loud, and I never laugh out loud. You'll want to rest up before reading this one. And after. Thank you, Sam."

B Broadway Books
Available wherever books are sold • www.broadwaybooks.com

ANNOUNCING THE 2002 PEN/ROBERT BINGHAM FELLOWSHIPS FOR WRITERS

Call for nominations from writers, editors and agents
Three two-year fellowships, each $35,000 a year

Three PEN/Robert Bingham Fellowships for Writers (each $35,000 a year for two consecutive years) will honor exceptionally talented fiction writers whose debut work – a first novel or collection of short stories published in 2000 or 2001 – represents distinguished literary achievement and suggests great promise.

Nominations are welcome by January 15, 2002, from writers, editors, literary agents, and members of the literary community. Describe the literary character of the candidate's work, and the degree of promise evident in his or her first book of literary fiction. Send three copies of the candidate's book with nomination. To be eligible, candidate's first (and only the first) novel or collection of short fiction must have been published by a U. S. trade publisher between January 1, 2000, and December 31, 2001. Candidates must be U. S. residents; American citizenship not required.

Winners must undertake and complete a project of public literary service that brings authors and their works to settings outside the literary mainstream, such as schools, adult educational programs, and literacy centers that serve low-income communities. These projects will be conducted under the auspices of PEN (www.pen.org).

Enquiries & nominations to:
PEN/Robert Bingham Fellowships for Writers,
PEN American Center
568 Broadway
New York, NY 10012
or via e-mail to: **jm@pen.org**

The Fellowships have been established by the family of Robert Bingham
to commemorate his contributions to literary fiction.

OPEN CITY

EDITORS
Thomas Beller
Daniel Pinchbeck

MANAGING EDITOR
Joanna Yas

ART DIRECTOR
Nick Stone

EDITOR-AT-LARGE
Adrian Dannatt

CONTRIBUTING EDITORS
Lee Ann Brown
Sam Brumbaugh
Vanessa Chase
Amanda Gersh
Laura Hoffmann
Kip Kotzen
Sam Lipsyte
Jim Merlis
Parker Posey
Elizabeth Schmidt
Alexandra Tager
Jon Tower
Tony Torn
Lee Smith
Piotr Uklanski
Jocko Weyland

EDITORIAL ASSISTANT
Alicia Bergman

COPY EDITOR
Jennifer Stroup

READERS
Gabriel Marc Delahaye
Matt Marinovich
Michael Panes
Micah Toub

FOUNDING PUBLISHER
Robert Bingham

Open City *is published triannually by Open City, Inc., a not-for-profit corporation. Donations are tax-deductible to the extent allowed by the law. A one-year subscription (3 issues) is $30; a two-year subscription (6 issues) is $55. Make checks payable to: Open City, Inc., 225 Lafayette Street, Suite 1114, New York, NY 10012. For credit-card orders, see our Web site: www.opencity.org. E-mail: editors@opencity.org.*

Front cover: "4 Times Square, 10/2/01"; back cover: "New Jersey Boatyard, 10/2/01." From the Phantom Towers Project by Julian LaVerdiere and Paul Myoda. Photography by Roe Ethridge.

Front page drawing by John Körmeling.

ISBN 1-890447-27-7
ISSN 1089-5523

Have a brief encounter with GRANTA MAGAZINE—free.

ReadyMade

PREVIEW ISSUE   INSTRUCTIONS FOR EVERYDAY LIFE

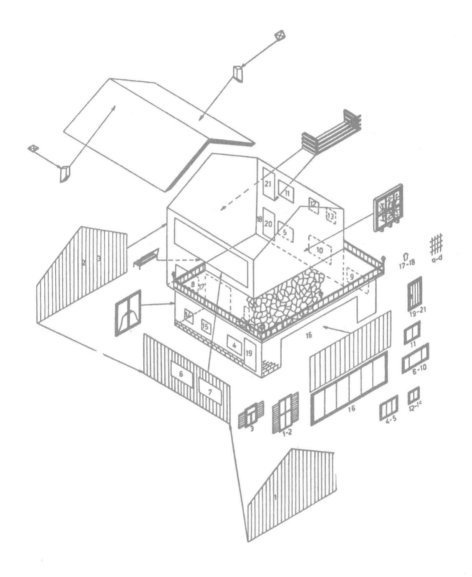

CONTRIBUTORS' NOTES

ROSA ALCALÁ, originally from Paterson, New Jersey, has translated Cecilia Vicuña's *El Templo* (Situations Press, 2001), *Cloud-Net* (Art in General, 1999), and *Word & Thread* (Morning Star Publications, 1996). Her own poems have recently appeared in *Chain* and *The World*. She is currently pursuing a PhD in English at SUNY-Buffalo, where she co-curates ñ: poesía, crítica, y arte, the university's non-unilingual reading series.

LOUISE BELCOURT is a painter who lives and works in Brooklyn. She most recently showed at Artemis · Greenberg Van Doren · Gallery in New York City, and Galerie 5ème Étage in Paris.

DODIE BELLAMY's books include *Feminine Hijinx* (Hanuman, 1990), *Real* (with Sam D'Allesandro, Talisman House, 1990), and *The Letters of Mina Harker* (Hard Press, 1998). *Cunt-Ups* is her newest publication (Tender Buttons, 2001).

NICO BAUMBACH is a writer living in Manhattan. This is his first published story.

ANSELM BERRIGAN is the author of *Integrity & Dramatic Life* and the forthcoming *Zero Star Hotel*, both from Edge Books. "Something like ten million . . ." was written for a Poetry Project reading on October 3, 2001, entitled "New Poems to End Greed, Imperialism, Opportunism, and Terrorism."

HAKIM BEY is the author of *T.A.Z.: The Temporary Autonomous Zone* (Autonomedia).

MICHAEL BROWNSTEIN is the author of three novels, *Country Cousins*, *Self-Reliance*, and *The Touch*, as well as several collections of stories and poetry. His next book, *World on Fire*, will be published by Open City Books in May 2002.

CRAIG CHESTER was born in the late mid-1960s. As an actor, he has appeared in ten independent films, including *Swoon*, *I Shot Andy Warhol*, and *Kiss Me, Guido*, and has also written two screenplays, *Save Me* and *Drama Kings*. His adventures traversing the homophobic waters of Hollywood as an openly gay actor have led to a regular column in *Instinct*, which then led to a book deal with St. Martin's Press. His first collection of essays, *Why the Long Face?*, will be published in June 2002.

BRENDA COULTAS is the author of *Early Films* and *A Summer Newsreel*. She has a book forthcoming from Coffeehouse Press in 2003. She is currently writing about the Bowery.

PETER CULLEY lives in South Wellington, British Columbia. His books include *The Climax Forest* and *Natural History*. His writings on visual art have appeared in numerous publications worldwide.

RENÉ DANIËLS was born in Eindhoven, the Netherlands, in 1950. He had major solo exhibitions at Metro Pictures in New York, Stedelijk Museum in Amsterdam, and the Basel Kunsthalle. He was also included in Documenta Seven (1982), and Nine (1992). Considered one of the most important post-war Dutch painters, he characterized his work as: "A search for the no-man's land between literature, art, and life." A stroke suffered in 1987 has prevented him from painting since then. He lives in Eindhoven.

STACY DORIS's books include *Paramour* (Krupskaya, 2000), *Kildare* (Roof, 1995), and *La vie de Chester Steven Wiener écrite par sa femme* (P.O.L., 1998), *Chroniques New Yorkaises,* (P.O.L., 2000). Just out from Potes & Poets is *Conference,* from which "Flight" is excerpted.

ELIZABETH GROVE is a writer and editor living in Brooklyn. She did work in a psychoanalytic training institute, but not in the basement.

NOY HOLLAND's first book of stories, *The Spectacle of the Body*, was published by Knopf. She is married to the writer Sam Michel; they live in a small hill town with their two children.

AMY HILL is a painter living in New York.

LISA JARNOT is the author of *Some Other Kind of Mission* and *Ring of Fire*. She lives in New York City and is writing a biography of Robert Duncan.

STEPHEN GRAHAM JONES has published stories in *Alaska Quarterly Review*, *Beloit Fiction Journal*, *Black Warrior Review*, *B&A*, *Cutbank*, *Flyway*, *Georgetown Review*, *Iconoclast, Quarterly West, South Dakota Quarterly*, and *Sundog*, among other journals. His first novel, *The Fast Red Road: A Plainsong*, was published by FC2 in 2000. He lives in Shallowater, Texas.

JOHN KÖRMELING was born in Amsterdam, the Netherlands, in 1951. An architect and artist, his major works include a house built on top of the customs office in Rotterdam, a drive-in ferris wheel in Utrecht, and a neon chandelier in the Schipol airport terminal. These drawings are from *Een Goed Book* (*A Good Book*), which was originally published by Centraal Museum Utrecht; a new edition will soon be released by Plug-In Gallery in Winnipeg, Canada.

HARRYETTE MULLEN is the author of four poetry books, most recently *Muse & Drudge* (Singing Horse, 1995). Two more books are forthcoming in February 2002: *Blues Baby: Early Poems* (Bucknell University Press), and *Sleeping With the Dictionary* (University of California Press). She teaches courses in American poetry, African-American literature, and creative writing at UCLA.

MAGGIE NELSON is the author of *Shiner*, a book of poems recently out from Hanging Loose Press (2001).

CYNTHIA NELSON doesn't live anywhere she stays, but she does go around. Try Louisville, Kentucky, the island Manhattan, or Northern California. Music she makes as she goes, with herself, Retsin, and The Naysayer. She has recorded and released six or seven albums. Her books of poetry with Soft Skull Press include *Raven Days* (1994) and *The Kentucky Rules* (1998). She is a cofounder of the *Fort Necessity* literary magazine

MICHIKO OKUBO is Japanese by birth. She grew up in Kyushu, the south of Japan, majored in French at the Tokyo University of Foreign Studies, and went on to study in England and France. She has lived in New York City and Hong Kong, and now lives in Tokyo. She finds it liberating to write in a second language.

SARAH PORTER was born in Michigan in 1969. She has lived an unsettled life, including spending a few years abroad in Budapest and Berlin. She came to Brooklyn looking for stability—she now works as an artists' model and has a small jewelry design business. She writes unpublished novels.

KEN SCHLES's new book, *The Geometry of Innocence*, is a haunting visual journey through contemporary urban life. His first book, *Invisible City*, was a *New York Times Book Review* selection of the year. He is challenged by the idea that we can transform the world into images that work as a reference point between individuals and he doesn't know anyone who would even think of sending him mail tainted with anthrax.

ROD SMITH is the author of *In Memory of My Theories* (O Books), *Protective Immediacy* (Roof), and, with Lisa Jarnot and Bill Luoma, *New Mannerist Tricycle* (Beautiful Swimmer). *The Good House*, a long poem, was recently published by Spectacular Books. He edits *Aerial* magazine, publishes Edge Books, and manages Bridge Street Books in Washington, DC.

BRIAN KIM STEFANS's books include *Free Space Comix*, *Gulf* and *Angry Penguins*. *Fashionable Noise: Digital Poetics* is forthcoming from Atelos Press. Several of his Web poems, including "The Dreamlife of Letters" and "The Truth Interview" (with Kim Rosenfield), can be found at ubu.com. He is a frequent contributor to *The Boston Review* and other publications.

CECILIA VICUÑA, Chilean poet and performer, lives between Chile and New York. Her most recent books are *El Templo*, translated by Rosa Alcala, (Situations, 2001), *Cloud-Net*, translated by Rosa Alcalá (Art in General, 1999), and *QUIPOem*, translated by Esther Allen (Wesleyan University Press, 1997).

ANNA

CLOTHES FOR WOMEN

150 E. 3rd Street at Ave. A
212.358.0195

photo by Hellin Kay

BRIDGE

STORIES AND IDEAS

ISSUE   NUMBER   THREE

Art Shay, John Barth, Vince Darmody, LD Beghtol, Rebecca Wolff, Patrick Welch, Wislawa Szymborska, Cris Mazza, Jim Munroe, Negativland, Gary Pike, Mike Topp, John Keene, Jon Langford, Frances Sherwood, Tim W. Brown, Mike Newirth, Wayne C. Booth, Lawrence Krauser, Joe Baldwin

WWW.BRIDGEMAGAZINE.ORG

THE GEOMETRY OF INNOCENCE

KEN SCHLES

Westcan
PRINTING GROUP

Our aim in business is very simple: to provide our customers with a top quality product and to always deliver what we have promised. To achieve this requires team effort – and over the years we have assembled one of the best teams in the industry – from administration through to production, our team of dedicated professionals genuinely care about each of the projects they undertake. We place the emphasis squarely where it belongs, upon the customer. We have long established the principle that our success depends on the success of our customers and therefore we will always do our utmost with each and every project.

We provide:

Competitive pricing, an efficient production schedule, exceptional quality and overall excellent value.

Proactive, knowledgable and friendly customer service from professionals who understand publishing and the needs of publishers.

A rewarding experience for all, we are passionate about what we do and are proud of the work we produce.

To learn more about us or to receive a quote on your next project, please call us toll free at 1+866.669.9914

84 Durand Road, Winnipeg, Manitoba, Canada R2J 3T2
Fax (204) 669-9920 • www.westcanpg.com

OPEN CITY

Open City *showcases the literature of tomorrow today.*
—Los Angeles Times

*An athletic balance of hipster glamour
and highbrow esoterica.*
—The Village Voice

Ambitiously highbrow.
—The New York Times

*Takes the old literary format and revitalizes
it for a new generation's tastes.*
—Library Journal

SUBSCRIBE

OPEN

Stories by Mary Gaitskill, Hubert Selby Jr., Vince Passaro. Art by Jeff Koons, Ken Schles, Devon Dikeou. (Vastly overpriced at $200, but fortunately we've had some takers. Only twenty-eight copies left.)

Stories by Martha McPhee, Terry Southern, David Shields, Jaime Manrique, Kip Kotzen. Art by Paul Ramirez-Jonas, Kate Milford, Richard Serra. (Ken Schles found the negative of our cover girl on 13th St. and Avenue B. We're still looking for the girl. $100)

Stories by Irvine Welsh, Richard Yates, Patrick McCabe. Art by Francesca Woodman, Jacqueline Humphries, Chip Kidd, Allen Ginsberg, Alix Lambert. Plus Alfred Chester's letters to Paul Bowles. (Our cover girl now has long brown hair. $150)

Stories by Cyril Connolly, Thomas McGuane, Jim Thompson, Samantha Gillison, Michael Brownstein, Emily Carter. Art by Julianne Swartz and Peter Nadin. Poems by David Berman and Nick Tosches. Plus Denis Johnson in Somalia. (A monster issue, sales undercut by slightly rash choice of cover art by editors. Get it while you can! $15)

CITY back issues

Make an investment in your future...
In today's volatile marketplace
you could do worse.

Change or Die
Stories by David Foster Wallace, Siobhan Reagan, Irvine Welsh. Jerome Badanes's brilliant novella, Change or Die (film rights still available). Poems by David Berman and Vito Acconci. Plus Helen Thorpe on the murder of Ireland's most famous female journalist, and Delmore Schwartz on T. S. Eliot's squint. (A must-have at only $17!)

The Only Woman He's Ever Left
Stories by James Purdy, Jocko Weyland, Strawberry Saroyan. Michael Cunningham goes way uptown. Poems by Rick Moody, Deborah Garrison, Monica Lewinsky, Charlie Smith. Art by Matthew Ritchie, Ellen Harvey, Cindy Stefans. Rem Koolhaas Project. With a beautiful cover by Adam Fuss. (Only $10 for this blockbuster. Free to the first six people who request it.)

The Rubbed Away Girl
Stories by Mary Gaitskill, Bliss Broyard, and Sam Lipsyte. Art by Jimmy Raskin, Laura Larson, and Jeff Burton. Poems by David Berman, Elizabeth Macklin, Steve Malkmus, and Will Oldham. (A reader from Queens chastises us for our shameful synergistic moment with indie rock. $10)

Beautiful to Strangers
Stories by Caitlin O'Connor Creevy, Joyce Johnson, and Amine Zaitzeff. Poems by Harvey Shapiro, Jeffrey Skinner, and Daniil Kharms. Art by Piotr Uklanski, David Robbins, Liam Gillick, and Elliott Puckette. Look for Zaitzeff's *Westchester Burning* in stores soon. ($10)

OPEN

Bewitched
Stories by Jonathan Ames, Said Shirazi, and Sam Lip-syte. Essays by Geoff Dyer and Alexander Chancellor, who hates rabbit. Poems by Chan Marshall and Edvard Munch on intimate and sensitive subjects. Art projects by Karen Kilimnick, Maurizio Cattelan, and M.I.M.E. (Oddly enough, our bestselling issue. $10)

Editors' Issue
Previously demure editors publish themselves. Enor-mous changes at the last minute. Stories by Robert Bingham, Thomas Beller, Daniel Pinchbeck, Joanna Yas, Adrian Dannatt, Kip Kotzen, Amanda Gersh, Jocko Weyland. Poems by Tony Torn. Art by Nick Stone, Meghan Gerety, and Alix Lambert. ($10)

Octo Ate Them All
Vestal McIntyre emerges from the slush pile like aphrodite with a brilliant story that corresponds to the tattoo that covers his entire back. Siobhan Reagan thinks about strangulation. Fiction by Melissa Pritchard and Bill Broun. Anthropologist Michael Taus-sig's Cocaine Museum. Gregor von Rezzori's medita-tion on solitude, sex, and raw meat. Art by Joanna Kirk, Sebastien de Ganay, and Ena Swansea.($10)

Equivocal Landscape
Sam Brumbaugh in Kenya, Daphne Beal and Swamiji, Paula Bomer sees red on a plane, Heather Larimer hits a dog, and Hunter Kennedy on the sexual possibilties of Charlottesville versus West Texas. Ford Madox Ford on the end of fun. Poetry by Jill Bialosky and Rachel Wetzsteon. Art by Miranda Lichtenstein and Pieter Schoolwerth; a love scene by Toru Hayashi. Mungo Thomson passes notes. ($10)

CITY back issues

Hi-fi

Sam Lipsyte enters The Special Cases Lounge, Nick Tosches smokes with God. Jack Walls remembers the gangs of Chicago, Vince Passaro ponders adult content. Poetry by Honor Moore, Sarah Gorham, and Melissa Holbrook Pierson. Mini-screenplay by Terry Southern. Art by Luisa Kazanas, Peter Pinchbeck, and Julianne Swartz. Special playwright section guest edited by Tony Torn. ($10)

ISSUE # 13 — OPEN CITY

go ahead and sing
your public thirst
(Cynthia Nelson, page 169)

The Blood of Familiar Objects

Sarah Porter

IT'S ALWAYS BEEN MY SISTER CLARA'S JOB TO DO THE BREATHING. As soon as I walk through the door she starts in at once, seizing and expelling air in rapid gasps as if she had just started up from a dream in which she couldn't breathe at all. I know, of course, that before I came in she was silent, and that she's begun panting like that only for my benefit; I'm at the end of all her efforts, I think at once, I'm what she wants to inhale. She won't slow down until she's positive that she's drawn me, breath by breath, back into the cycling rituals of our childhood, until she's made sure that I remember everything and that I can't stop remembering. Then she smiles at me, as an invitation to pretend with her that all that labor was just a game, and I smile back to placate her, because I know that she won't stop until I do. I can't stand to listen to her hyperventilating like that; it's a deformation of the gentle, metronomic way she always used to breathe when we were children, when the sound coming from her was a kind of subliminal pillowing constantly in the air at my side. I fell asleep to that soft sound, I kept it close to me all the time I was awake, and if I couldn't hear her I felt certain that I would suffocate. It was beautiful, the way she breathed, until it became a performance, and now the self-consciousness of it has made it tawdry and painful. Clara looks at me and sees how she's sucked me back into the old rhythms, and thinks that she's triumphed over me. She thinks that she's drawn me firmly into a past where nothing can change, as if her breathing were a room in which none of the furniture had been moved and all the birds were still safely locked inside their cages. The smile she gives me is anxious and complacent at the same time. She's recited the past so well that now it surrounds us both, but she doesn't recognize that within it everything has altered and become slightly grotesque. The birds are just where she wants them to be, but their heads have grown bulbous and so heavy that there is no more possibility of flight. She's right to believe that she's breathed me so securely into our old ways that I can't get out, she wins every time, but what she doesn't know is that the past can only talk about one thing, and that's how many things will never be the same again.

I let the door fall shut behind me, and I go up and embrace her with my smile carefully bouncing complicity back into hers; it's easier that way. The furniture of the old parlor is upholstered in red velvet just like it always was; I pull an armchair close to her place on the sofa, still smiling. Here and there the velvet is damp with open sores, but I sit on it anyway without saying anything. The birds are all fast asleep with their weighted heads tilted down onto their shoulders, and nothing is singing above the drowsy percussion of the radiator. Clara leaves the room to make us coffee. The air of the parlor is thicker without her to disturb it, and the dull smell of blood hovers undispersed; by leaving me alone with this listless stench she would like to bring me to accept that her breathing is better than nothing, at least in such a close space. There were never any windows in this house, or if there were then the walls grew in and sealed them over long ago. Maybe I can just barely remember a time when there were still a few naked patches of glass shining blue with the sweet expansiveness of the day beyond, and maybe if I got up from the chair and searched I might find places where the ivory shutters that encased them are still faintly distinguishable from the spread of the plaster. Clara, I would like to say, why am I the visitor in this house? But as she comes back in with the coffee and pallid rolls on a tray I can see her face straining slightly from the pressure of a gentle, frightened impulse to trust me, and I can't bring myself to hurt her like that. She doesn't need to be reminded that she has never left here, that she keeps her blood in a tender and continuous interchange with the blood that swells out the deep red upholstery. My clothes are still cold with the wildness of the air beyond the house; Clara must have felt that when I leaned over to hug her, and that in itself is a brutal suggestion of too many things unknown to her. The coffee adds a charred note to the sour flavor crowded in between the walls. I had almost forgotten the walls, but now I see them much too clearly, covered in bubbly ochre paper and as sticky as fresh sap.

Clara seats herself again on the sofa, on a spot where the velvet is especially raw and seeping, her movements lavishly casual, the clear still beauty of her blonde face floating with deliberate remoteness between the ashy falls of her hair. Her smile moves in dreamy isolation from her other features. The silky obliviousness of her manner starts to irritate me, and I feel a terrible impulse to rip into it, to force her to pay attention. I say, Clara, how have Mom and Dad been? And as soon as I ask this a scraping starts up in the ceiling immediately above us, just as if my words had forcibly dragged the source of that noise into being. Clara jerks up with her mouth distending slightly before she composes herself again, reducing down into a pale curl. Neither of us really knows anymore if the commotion in the ceiling is generated by something that could in fact be our parents, and Clara turns on me with eyes too sad with a sleepy opacity to quite be called reproachful; still, she holds them on mine in silence long enough to make it clear that my playacting has pushed too far. She's much too loyal, though, to leave me alone with such a hazardous question, and after another minute she says, Mom and Dad? Oh, they've been pretty good. She says, I mean they seem peaceful, but of course neither of them remembers very much anymore, not in the way that you or I can still remember things. Their bedroom is just very empty, she says, really almost nothing in there at all. I know just what Clara is implying by this. She means, don't you see how together you and I can remember so much? This room, this deep velvet, the occasional somnolent disturbance of the birds; isn't it all wonderful? She's demanding, I know, that I not abandon her again inside the ramifications of so much memory, clotted and luxuriant on every side; she hates it when I go away. The room feels very close, and we both look up at once at the place where a sudden chandelier sheds revolutions of heavy light.

I can't help resenting her expectation; the truth is that I would like to forget everything in this room, really, even though my forgetting would leave Clara feeling desperately alone. In my exasperation I start needling at her. Clara, I say, how can you be sure they don't remember everything in here just as well as we do? Do you ever try to really sit down and talk to them about it? Mom especially, I tell her, I bet Mom might surprise you if you gave her a chance sometime; she's always been way more sensitive than she usually lets on. That chandelier, I say, the way all that light drips down as if it were crying: that looks just like the kind of thing Mom would talk about if anybody ever took the time to draw her out. She's just shy. Even as the words are emerging from me I know that it's dangerous, and even stupid, for me to speak of those noises as if they had a personality, to grant them the substance of a name, let alone their own sensibility. But I can't stop myself; just once I want to hear Clara say to me, You fucking know there's no one up there! I want to goad her into saying, How can you possibly rattle on about parents, when there's never been anyone here but the two of us? I keep wanting her to admit it, even as the noises in the ceiling begin ordering themselves into a monotony of footsteps.

Clara won't, of course, allow me to lure her into saying anything so far beyond the bounds of safety, but she starts breathing again with a tubercular vehemence, ruffling up the sediment of illness that covers the furniture. We both hear how measured and distinct the footsteps in the ceiling have become now, how confidently human, and all because I had to go and encourage them. They must have heard my voice creeping up from the ruby depths of the parlor, heard me call them Mom, and so now they feel entitled to shape themselves accordingly; it really sounds just as if there actually were such a person, living out a passive and ordinary life in some inconceivable room above us. Clara can't keep her beautiful eyes blinded enough to conceal her anger; she almost leers at me, and even I start to feel afraid of whatever it is up there that my voice has set in motion. I'm terrified that Clara will turn against me with the words, Well, then wouldn't you like to go up and visit with them for a while? It sounds like they're awake. She doesn't do it, Clara is almost never cruel, but our eyes meet and the fear of everything she could say to me glissades back and forth between us in a kind of airy transfusion. We know each other so well that she can simply curl deeper into the sofa, her slim milky body contracting into something hardly wider than a satin ribbon, and let the footsteps and the light moving between our eyes speak for her, in the assurance that I can only understand her perfectly.

In fact the rainy weight of the footsteps above us is already saying far too much. Now that I've stopped my talk about our parents it seems to me that the noises should start to subside, but instead they go on, gaining in vigor and certainty, and then Clara and I both jump at what sounds like an awkward bulk groping its way onto the stairs. The stairs creak terribly, one by one, as some immense and shapeless burden patiently lowers itself toward the parlor. I break down before she does: Clara, I say, is it going to stop in time? She waits for a moment as if she hadn't heard me; I can't believe that she would leave me suspended in such awful fear. Then she says, I know Mom has forgotten about all this, because the last time she came down here everything just disappeared, all that was left was like this hard bare space, you couldn't even tell if it was shaped like a room at all anymore. It was something but not quite even a room, and everything in it kept moving all the time. What are you saying? I ask. The last time she came down? In a frantic effort to stop the noises from coming any closer, I say, But Mom can't even walk anymore, you know she can't walk! For an instant it seems to me that the noises have understood me; a slight hesitation interrupts the rhythm of their descent. But then Clara smiles in a way I've never seen before, rippling up her lovely face into a sequence of unquiet pleats, and says something reckless and awful into the compact air: But, she tells me, but I told you she's been feeling better lately. Clara can't seem to stop smiling and her face purls with an unsettled malice. She says, I hated it, I had to live like that for weeks, down between all these naked little oscillating walls. One reason I've been looking forward to you coming is I figured it would help get the house back together again. It worked, she says, it worked for a few minutes, anyway; the chandelier even came back for a second, I was so impressed with you! So do you think I should be grateful for what I could get?

I'm so astonished that at first I say nothing; in embarrassment my eyes crawl away from her and up into the ceiling. Above me are brittle gleams that seem to have twisted free from the chandelier and infested the corners with a murky, opalescent glittering. I try to remember what there is on the far side of that ceiling, where a new legion of sounds is shuffling in and out of focus; it's obvious to me now that I must, of course, have been upstairs many times. It even seems to me Clara and I shared a bedroom up there when we were small children, but in my mind all the spaces above have worn down into formlessness; I can't get a handle on them. Clara, I say, what did Mom look like? Did you actually see her? Did she look like a regular person at all? The questions flurry out of my mouth with a hideous unrestraint and Clara's breathing shoves around me like the jostling of cloudy, enormous bodies. Clara has started laughing, I realize it now, and that's what gives her breathing such a jagged force. She says, Your memory is going pretty selective, isn't it, if you can't even put Mom together anymore? I've been giving you too much credit, I guess, just because you remember this room. Even the room gets a little sicker every time you come over. Clara can't stop laughing, and the walls look slippery and disjointed at the corners, loosened by the pressure of her laughter. Clara, I say, stop it right now! I say, I bet you don't remember Mom either, you don't even know if there was ever anybody like that at all, not anywhere in our house! I can't quite locate Clara any longer, but I catch the look in her eyes even without seeing her face; her eyes are pasty with secrets. She lets me feel the density of everything she knows and keeps on withholding it from me, until I can't help but recognize the truth of what she's been saying. My voice is losing its strength as I say, Clara, but how can you possibly remember something I don't? You grew up inside of everything I've ever known, there's nothing for you outside here! I'm the one who's been living outside, and she answers, Well then you should realize that certain things must have come back to us in your absence. That's the risk you take going away, you know, that we have time to do some recollecting without your being here to try and stop us. By now her voice is so disfigured by laughter that I can't recognize it.

My back is drenched with the secretions of the armchair, I feel that much clearly, but I've lost track of the walls. I think that my fear must be obvious to Clara, that because of me the contours of the room must be pulsing much too quickly, because I can sense her queasy amusement. Clara says, I've been upstairs quite a bit recently, it looks a lot like this. Mom can't remember what walls are like, but she still knows some other things, she's been telling me all kinds of stories. She's been telling me lots of stuff about when you were a kid; she said that even back then the birds were fine as long as you weren't in the room with them, but as soon as you got home from school or whatever they would start to get sick. Mom even told me that you wouldn't remember how you were the one who always made them sick; it's funny, you know, I actually tried to defend you, but now I can see that she understands you a lot better than you understand her! Clara is right that I can't remember ever having made the birds get sick, I can't remember the birds at all; now and then I catch a gleam from the brass of their cages, but I'm sure that the cages themselves have suddenly emptied. Mom told me, Clara says, that she couldn't stand to see them like that, so diseased that they could hardly move around their cages, and that's why we had to put them under.

Under what? I ask, though I don't really expect Clara to be able to hear what I say anymore. I realize that there is nothing definite in the room at all now, no thick carnal upholstery, no sad flecks of light from the chandelier. Clara says, We had to bury the sofa too, it kept bleeding. She says, It is cleaner, having the room like this, even if it makes me kind of lonely sometimes.

and the city opened up as if to apologize

for its heat and changing ways

(Maggie Nelson, page 179)

The Glass Garden

Michiko Okubo

IT IS DARK AND BARE IN THE RESTAURANT. A LUNCHTIME CROWD
is thinning out fast, the echo of their hushed voices settling like dregs
in the stark interior. At the corner table Yasushi toys with the business
card of a jeweler his colleague has recommended. "Call them first.
They'll steer your fiancée within your range. They're very discreet."
As if rehearsing a visit, his lips quiver imperceptibly. They are not
thick but wide and fluid, rather out of place in his clean, angular face.

He managed to sleep for a few hours on the plane back to Tokyo,
but dull pain is just settling in his eyes and the pit of his stomach. He
glances at his wristwatch. It's 4:50 A.M. in London, he calculates. He
looks at the door: there are ten more minutes before his lunch
appointment with Reiko. His eyes rest on an old woman sitting alone.
There is an unoccupied table between hers and Yasushi's. She cocks
her white head at a waitress and orders sake. He is surprised to hear
her voice: she seems so complete in her detachment. She flicks open
a small fan and holds it in front of her throat where the triangular
opening of her kimono has exposed it.

He turns to the sound of water. Behind his table is a glass-fronted
alcove fitted into the wall, a miniature courtyard. Water fills a bamboo trough that balances precariously, like a seesaw, over the rock
basin. The dark gravel sucks in the sunlight from above, and on the
lithe bamboo tree leaves quiver in a breeze. He taps at the jeweler's

card, rolling his fiancée's name on his tongue. *Re-i-ko, Re-i-ko.* Again his eyes wander to the door. At any moment it will bring her in and she the light. For now the latticed windows all but shut off the light from the street. The rust orange walls, the stone floor, and the dark wood tables recede into darkness; the darkness is kept as deliberately as the light of the day caught in the glass garden. A Japanese garden in a closet—he can't decide if he likes the idea. He flips through the menu, brush and ink on rice paper. He slaps it shut. Today is going to be one of those days when he vacillates endlessly.

The old woman hovers at the periphery of his vision. Her kimono is the pale blue of winter dusk. A wide sash clamps her torso, but she seems as free as the air she stirs with her fan. He can almost smell sandalwood emanating from the delicate fan. She sits slightly at an angle to the table, oblique, as if it were her way of dealing with life. Restraint and nonchalance, he wonders what sets these women of the night apart: he is certain she belongs to that mysterious species. The woman closes the fan with two hands and inserts it under the sash and over her heart. She lifts the white porcelain flask by the neck and pours the clear liquid into a tiny cup. Not a single movement is wasted, her upright posture intact. The edge of the cup touches her lips and a color spreads on her cheeks, making her look like a young woman. Her private show begins, her own and for herself. Yasushi gets the sensation of a warm current of sake flowing down his throat, conjuring memories of the woman, the memories unknown and unknowable. He half closes his eyes.

One spring he watched three young women pass under his bed-room window, every day around four o'clock. He was thirteen, in bed with bronchitis. He kept peering into the darkening streets, but he never saw them come back his way. Not long after that he was in a car waiting for his mother. A recurring fever and a scent of daphne through the open window made him dizzy. He gazed up at the hazy sky, and then pressed his head on the door frame, pinning his restless mind. The breeze grazed his temple, fluffing his hair, and he lifted his face for more. Then he saw. The side mirror was filled with three women in embroidered kimonos, their faces powdered and their hair done up in elaborate knots. The figures grew bigger and soon overflowed the mirror, as the breeze laid a new smell over the fragrance of daphne. He curled up in the seat, peeking over the frame. One by one the women shuffled past, just a few inches from the car, so close that they smothered him with their mysterious scent. He breathed through his mouth a few times and cautiously leaned out the window. It was only then that he realized they were the young women who had passed under his bedroom window. He stared at their receding backs and thought of warriors in full armor marching to a battle. He sat back, pleased with this association: it somehow explained to him their transformation. The knots of their sashes swayed on their backs, the hems of their kimonos flared, and they vanished around the corner. He licked his dry lips, and then swallowed; the empty corner conjured up his mother. He gripped the edge of the seat. The door opened on the driver's side and his mother's scent floated in, clean and sharp. She asked him how he was feeling, but said nothing about the geishas. He edged away from his mother to guard his secret.

The sliding door rattles open. In the doorway Reiko stands, framed in the sunlight: her body phosphorescent, her face blurred. An alien, he thinks, for a fleeting second. She waves and steps out of the halo, metamorphosing into a human. He stands up, blinking. She is upon him in a flash, her smile cutting sideways her oval face. He goes round the table to pull a chair out for her.

"No. I'll sit here. It's more intimate."

Reiko bounces onto a chair nearer to him, the one on his left. She likes sitting this way, he remembers, now showing her profile, then three-quarters of her face. Elbows on the table, she cups her chin in her hands and looks into his eyes, confident of her worth and of his love. A whiff of her young sweat tickles his nose, the smell of boiled milk. It dispels the fragile scent of sandalwood from his mind.

Lightly he strokes Reiko's cheek, brushing off his dismay with his fingertips. Her skin feels moist and downy. She crinkles her nose like a schoolgirl. Then she snatches his finger, holds it between her lips, the tip of her tongue teasing. Her tanned body flares up in his memory and the blood surges, but the tug ebbs prematurely.

She bites his finger before releasing it. "You missed me, did you?"

He clasps her hands in his, stifling her question. What if he pulls her up on his knees and slips his hand between her thighs? Just to see if he gets rock hard. The need is urgent: he must know. Instead he orders beer and grips her hands tightly, crushing his panic. He tries to revive the thrill he felt when he called her from his hotel room in London, but only dry scraps of conversations pop up at random. In his hands, the joints of her fingers grow more distinct against him palms; chill clings to the back of his neck like a wet cloth. He wishes to be alone, utterly alone like the old woman in the pale kimono, if only for a few minutes. Reiko's face glows, unblemished by self-doubts. Awful tenderness creeps up on him, the first intimation of guilt.

Reiko withdraws her hands, wrinkling her nose again, and opens the menu. "I'm starving." Confident he would miss the touch of her hands, so confident she was compelled to explain.

He smoothes an involuntary curl off the corner of his lips. A sharp, clear sound reverberates in the glass garden, the bamboo trough hitting the rock basin. He looks up, thinking of the brimming trough toppling. The solitary woman is holding him in her steady gaze. No, she is watching the bamboo trough. A waitress cuts in his vision, severing their silent exchange with her back. Maybe the old woman was watching the waitress approaching her table. She picks up the bill and gets up. All in one motion, swift and precise. With such self-possession she no longer needs an armor. She is her own creation, her independence absolute, for she owes nothing to the world. Her hand on the sliding door, she turns her head slightly. Is she really looking at him? Scorn or pity, he can't read her face. How impertinent, he bristles inside. Why, she is only a woman of pleasure. His grudging admiration for her hard-won dignity turns sour.

Her kimono burns white in the sunlight, then she is gone. He breathes more easily.

"A fossil of a geisha," Reiko whispers. "You can always tell, can't you? Once dipped in the water trade, you're stained for life, they say."

"Water trade," or "the world of flowers and willows," as Yasushi's father prefers to call it. Or simply "those people," as his mother will say, spitting the words sideways, as if to avoid contamination.

"Serving men all your life." Reiko shudders. "I can't think of any more degrading way to live."

She tosses another glance at the vacated table.

"No more degrading than being on stage." There is a note of irritation in his low voice.

"They're dying out anyway. I'm glad of that," she says casually.

"They aren't so different from us."

"Don't be silly."

"We all have to serve one way or another to earn our existence," he insists. Why is he defending the old woman drinking alone in the middle of the day? He looks around as if for an answer. The darkness has slackened; the light in the garden has dulled in contrast.

"You're in a funny mood." She lays her hand on his arm, while redirecting her eyes to the menu. "You can't take them seriously. They are like, like . . . anyway, they don't really belong."

Sure they don't belong, they don't count, but do I belong? Where do you or any of us belong? The bamboo trough hits the basin again. The sound startles him.

The crisp batter of tempura cracks between Reiko's white teeth, a small mound of rice on the black lacquered chopsticks disappears through her red lips. The sight of her eating always fascinates Yasushi, her appetite for life and matter-of-fact way in fulfilling it. It even arouses a sensual pleasure.

She chatters away as if she were the one who had been away, not he. About jealousy she inspires in her colleagues, particularly in Miss Kato, a dry woman of thirty-five, about her aerobics class, about her latest purchases. She fires away with the urgency of one trying to stretch time by cramming it with words. Her words wash over him. She widens and narrows her eyes, purses her lips, and flips back her hair—never in repose. As if he were a mirror, he twists his neck slightly, letting her eyes glide off his face. Her words come out unexamined and her expressions unchecked; innocence, ignorance or arrogance, what is she? She claims an unreserved right to happiness, but a right unearned, he protests. Will she swell like her mother or harden like his as years go by?

"Is Rome better than Vienna? We could do both, couldn't we? Paris, too. But then I won't get to see Florence," she says, her mouth glistening with grease.

"What, Florence?" He holds on to the word he has caught.

"We'd better start planning now, you know. Not so much of the trip itself, but . . ."

Just then a shadow of uncertainty flickers across her face. Even earlier there might have been signs of nervousness and vulnerability. If only he had stopped to look more carefully . . . Weariness steals over him, only jet lag.

The darkness of the restaurant has lost its urgency: the old geisha has taken away the mystery. He mourns the loss. In that textured darkness he could see more clearly. Through the lattice the light is trickling down by stealth. Yasushi thrusts his hand into his pants pocket and crumples the card of the jeweler. He makes no plan. He decides he rather likes the daylight trapped in the glass garden. It is contained, and that is all he can manage for now.

Guilty Pleasure

Nico Baumbach

SINCE I WAS A CHILD—AND I NEVER REALLY WAS, WHICH IS WHY I kind of still am—I have always felt that if I wanted to apply myself to a problem, I mean really apply myself, I would invariably be able to conquer it. The catch is *wanting* to apply myself. Because as soon as I approach something that is not clearly within my grasp, I no longer want it. I could of course apply myself to this problem, but do I really want to? Well yes, I do, but in a minute, not right now. Just get off my back and I'll get to it, I swear.

The immediate problem was with my schoolwork. I'll explain. I'll explain this and then I'll get to Cecilia. I was in my junior year of college and I wasn't working and was not doing well and not happy about that. Meanwhile, my two pretty close friends were away—junior year abroad. I'd thought about J.Y.A., seemed like a good opportunity—be in a foreign place, gain distance and perspective, and then change irrevocably, leaving everyone else behind. But somehow I failed to ever commit to a plan. It meant choosing a country and a program and, well, I never did; so here I was, back at school, trying to reassure myself with a new plan. The new plan was that while everyone else was off in foreign lands seeing the world with new eyes, I was going to take advantage of being free from distractions, to bear down, isolate myself, and focus on my work.

But in November, two months after the semester started, the plan seemed not really to have gone into effect. For one thing, the total lack of contact with friends, people calling me, people to make plans with, far from releasing me from distraction, was making me more lonely and restless. The truth is, even when I had friends around, it was more the idea of socializing that often kept me from work, the idea that I should be doing more; my plan should really have been to not complain or worry about the fact that I was always pretty isolated anyway. I lived in a nook in a mostly freshman dorm, called "singles row," a hallway of upper classmen living by themselves. I had imagined it might be an interesting group, others like myself, who have little interest in living in suites with their best buddies and partying every night and so sought silence and concentration, discipline. But, by the looks of things, they were an odd collection of losers, most of whom would probably rather be having parties in suites every night with their best buddies were that option still available. In other words, others like myself.

Then there was the problem of my classes. Part of what discipline means to me is learning things I feel are important. This means history and science. History because I want to be knowledgeable about the world, to have a wealth of facts at my fingertips, to have a sense of scope and the processes of change, and when some reference is made, to be able to know and explain the history and shed new light on the object in question. Science because I want to know how things work, to understand the mechanics of the physical and biological world, and to explain them to those for whom the world is still a shady place of chance and coincidence. The idea was never to become a historian or a scientist, but to be a repository of knowledge, which I would then use for other means, whatever those may be.

But while I had liked the idea of knowing stuff, I'd never wanted to learn it. Or at least, I was proving to have no memory for names, dates, formulas, and theories. This was why I had avoided these subjects before—a possibility since this reputable college wasn't stuffy but enlightened, and prided itself on offering its student body the responsibility that comes with freedom. This allowed you to stick within your comfort zone, while still knowing that you were participating in this great liberal education, as if options not taken were still options. My comfort zone—mostly English classes—of course was never very comfortable, and so I was comforted by not taking what I would have been comfortable taking.

I had fulfilled my plan insofar as I would go to the lectures and discussion groups. I never missed a class. If nothing else, being present could count toward the fulfillment of my regimen. Though I absorbed nothing, I still had some minor sense of accomplishment and secretly I suppose I believed that somehow I was learning against all evidence to the contrary. Like people who buy a tape to increase their vocabulary, and play it while they are sleeping. I hoped that somewhere in the recesses of my mind there was learning taking place that would some day make itself known. So, while as I sat in class, with the hundreds of other students—nothing on the surface separating me from them—furiously scribbling notes, my mind would wander, occasionally picking up on some word or phrase that seemed to be stressed, which I would write in my notebook: "the telophase of meiosis 1." It would offer a key to that knowledge which I would decipher at a later date—a date that was endlessly deferred.

Okay, stage set, now to get to Cecilia. Well, first I have to start with Jack. I had not liked Jack from the moment I saw him. A guy who lived down the hall who sort of stuck out for me, who came to somehow represent what I didn't like about people who lived in the hall. He was stocky, only about 5' 5", baggy jeans that swallowed up his squat legs, a wallet chain, a hoop earring in each ear, short spiky hair and a pockmarked face. Ugly, I thought—not in a sad lonely way (good), but in a cocky way (bad). I have respect for a restrained sort of coolness, but none for dudes who just want a good time. But as I kept an eye on him—because he irritated me so, he was the guy I paid the most attention to—it seemed that he didn't have so many good times. I'd often see him reading in the lounge on a Friday or Saturday night. And, as it happened, perhaps because he saw me watching him, he developed the habit of nodding Hi to me. And I of course nodding back.

It turned out that I started to at least not dislike Jack. His attitude was far less aggressive than his appearance suggested. When he would nod Hi it wasn't with any necessary expectation of friendship, no eager smile, just matter-of-fact, and I appreciated that. Not a bad guy, Jack, and soon I found myself struggling to repress a smile on my face as I nodded Hi back to him, a smile that might betray the fact that yeah, I might not mind being friends with him.

One day, when I was playing music and had left my door ajar, he peered in.

"Porter, right?"

"Uh-huh."

"Jack. We have a class together. Is that Boulez conducting Schoenberg?"

I had to glance at the jewel box. "Yeah. You want to come in?"

He came in and sat on the bed. "This is the recording where . . ." And then we talked about some other stuff, not much really, not in much detail, and then he left.

But as it turned out it was the first of many similar visits. Jack would come in, always uninvited but not unwanted, flop down on the bed—the narrow room contained a single desk chair and a bed, so the latter was the only place for a visitor to sit—and maybe look through the CDs on the shelf above my bed. "Is this Leon Payne's demo version of 'Lost Highway'?" Jack did a radio show on the college station and he was interested in my willfully esoteric collection of music, endless inevitably failed gestures toward authenticity—oddball regional country western bands from the forties like the Rambling Rangers to avant-garde jazz, a lot of stuff that I knew little to nothing about, but accumulated with the sense that the collection itself counted for something like being an aficionado. Don't think I didn't know that obscurity is its own commodity; there are stores that sell only this stuff.

We'd chat a little about music or maybe movies or books, again not in much detail. "Yeah, I read that, it was good . . ." "Oh yeah? It was good?" "Yeah." "I should read it." Sometimes we wouldn't talk at all, he'd just hang out for a little while, both of us reading different things, until eventually he'd excuse himself and go back to his room. Generally, I welcomed his arrival. A relief, the comfort of another presence to keep me from getting too caught up in my own painfully circular thought process—the endless attempt to distract myself from distraction. But as soon as he settled in, I felt myself getting a little irritated. Here he was taking up my time and space, distracting me from my work. God knows what I could be accomplishing were he not here. But when he would get up to leave I would find myself disappointed and lonely again.

Okay, so Jack and I were in the same class. It was my one English class, my one softball, my one gift to myself in my schedule: The Modern American Novel. And we not only shared the same three-time-a-week lecture in an auditorium, but also the same discussion section once a week. The discussion section, the more intimate ten-person meeting that offered you the opportunity to strut your stuff— not for the professor herself, but for some uncomfortable graduate student who led the discussion. Jack—another reason I liked him— would, like me, sit silently each week, and would take an attitude toward stuff-strutting that seemed to waver between condescension and indifference, but was really about intense fear. Even as Jack's visits to my room became more and more frequent, we would still never share eye contact in section, both sitting nervously, as obscured as we could be in the not unintimate setting, hoping the discussion would never get stalled enough that the grad student would try a new tactic and call on one of us. I'm just assuming this is how Jack felt, he and I, two peas. Anyway there was this one girl in the section who I despised.

Cecilia. It wasn't her name I despised. Not a bad name, Cecilia, I suppose, at least not "common," the way this girl was common. A gross word, common, to describe a person. I am not quite so effete, but it fits only because I'd imagine that it is the last thing she'd want to be, and it fits because I despise the word itself. So I grew to despise the name Cecilia, as I despise the word "common," and the word "effete" too, for that matter, as I grew to despise her.

I'll try to describe her as I saw her back then. I'll try, but it's hard even writing about her. Not because I despised her, in fact I don't anymore, at least not in the same way I did then. But thinking about her back then, it makes me a little sick to my stomach. I'm not kidding, but here goes. She wasn't pretty. I think I can say that with some sense of popular opinion. She wasn't. But she did have really large breasts and she wasn't really heavy or anything, and so this fact, the really large (and I mean huge!) breasts and the fact that she wasn't fat gave her what might be thought of as a sexual aura that at any rate she seemed bent on capitalizing upon. Her back was always slightly arched, thrusting her chest forward, as if in an effort to point to it. No, not just to point to it, as if it needed pointing to, but to announce her own awareness of it. To point to, not just her chest itself, or even her awareness of it, but her awareness of your awareness of her awareness of it. A tacit vulgar dialogue she perpetually carried on with the rest of the world.

So this was her one asset, though really only an asset for the fetishists. 'Cause if we're really sizing her up, her chest was disproportionately large, making her seem nearly off balance. She was short, maybe about Jack's height, hips a little wide, and below the waist no curves to speak of. And the face, just round, pinched, and unpleasant.

Unlike Jack and myself, Cecilia had no fears about talking in section. If she had any fear, it was probably the fear of shutting up for one second, the fear that attention would at any moment leave her and her chest. She would dominate section, her high-pitched voice always a little louder than necessary, her pauses drawn out to allow each empty word to take up as much space as possible. Even when she wasn't talking, she dominated the room; you could feel her straining to contain herself, her back arching in impatience. While someone else was talking, we were all waiting for her to talk, if only to get it over with. She wasn't a bimbo or a ditz, I don't want to be creating that impression. Her comments were the result of some sort of concerted effort, an effort if not to understand the novel, then to say what she believed one was supposed to say about the novel. And it wasn't that she said stupid things, but she said obvious, uninteresting things, and said them as if they were the most important things in the world.

One evening when Jack was in my room, flopped on the bed, flipping through my *London Review of Books*, one of several subscriptions I received but rarely read, I brought up Cecilia. Not really as a subject for discussion, I just made some cracks about how irritating she was and mocked her monologue on Faulkner that we had suffered earlier that day. I had never mentioned Cecilia to Jack before, but I felt comfortable enough with him at this point that I assumed he would be on my side. He peered up from the newspaper and muttered, "Yeah, but you'd fuck her."

I was taken by surprise. I had never heard Jack mention girls or sex before—I assumed it was something that wasn't on his mind. I've never been much for this kind of guy conversation. The whole idea of two guys sitting around together using the word "fuck" as a verb makes me uneasy. Anyway, I didn't want to alienate Jack, and so I made what I thought to be a vague judicious comment: "I doubt it, but I guess it depends on the context."

As soon as I said it, I knew the word "context" was nerdy in this context; you don't follow up the word "fuck" with "context." But Jack played along: "My context may come tonight." He grinned a little, put down the paper, and proceeded to explain that, as it happened, that very day after class he and Cecilia had gotten into a conversation and apparently she was going to stop by his room later that night "to hang out and smoke some weed."

After Jack left, I couldn't stop thinking about him and Cecilia. I wasn't sure why exactly, but the whole idea of the date bothered me. Jack with Cecilia—it seemed preposterous. Now the reasons that Jack should know better than to be interested in Cecilia seemed obvious and endless. But Jack himself was not a handsome man and hardly Mister Personality; why Cecilia would take an interest in him seemed even more perplexing. Whether she deserved better may have been one question, but my assumption would have been that in certain superficial ways she would aim higher.

Don't get me wrong, I know I'm no prize. By denigrating Jack's currency with girls, I am in no way invested in elevating my own. But yeah, I guess if we really addressed the issue, I'd assumed I could pull something off that Jack couldn't. I'm sort of tall and lanky and a bit sickly looking, but I've always thought that the combination of my dark hair, blue eyes, and harsh features might give off the impression of depth. Sure, it might sound dubious, but once or twice I've even found some insecure girl to corroborate this theory. Anyway, it seemed to me that, given all of Cecilia's faults, Jack still seemed like an odd choice. And given that Jack would fuck her, I was hoping somewhere that she wouldn't be interested.

While trying to get some reading in a lengthy book on the Crusades done that evening, I took a couple of unnecessary trips to the communal kitchen just to pass by Jack's room and see if I could get a sense of what was going on in there. Either discretion or fear of being caught kept me from pressing my ear to the door, and so all I could make out was the faint sound of music coming through, one of my CDs that Jack had borrowed.

Jack didn't come by my room the next day, or the next. The third morning, as I opened my door, I saw Jack's door—four doors down from me—open, and out came Cecilia in a towel. She turned toward me for a moment, the towel, over her enormous breasts, forced to rise up in front, and I had the sense from about twenty feet away that I could see her pubic hair, but it could have just been shadow. She smiled, a sly welcoming smile that seemed both mocking and perhaps an invitation. I'm relying mostly on impression and memory here— this smile lasted not more than a couple of seconds—and she then turned the other direction and I watched her awkward stumpy legs head toward the women's bathroom.

In the early evening, Jack stopped by my room. Far from feeling the usual irritation once he had made himself comfortable, I found myself wanting him to stay. I couldn't escape the feeling that something had changed between us. That perhaps this visit was only out of courtesy, that somehow I had worn out my welcome. I played it poker-faced, and as it turned out, Jack too was convincingly the same as always. He didn't stay long that night, but the visits continued, maybe a little less regularly than they had been, but otherwise nothing had changed. We had our usual brief conversations. We just talked about music or books or whatever, made some bland jokes about another guy down the hall—my new least favorite—but mostly just hung out in the same space. He never mentioned Cecilia and neither did I.

In the section Jack and Cecilia and I shared, he and Cecilia never seemed to acknowledge each other, not unlike he and myself. But I would see Cecilia in our dorm stopping by Jack's room pretty often. I became attuned to the sounds in the hallway so I could peek out and see if someone might be walking by, naturally, as if maybe I was looking for someone. One day I peered out to see Cecilia knocking on Jack's door. As it happened, I knew Jack was at the radio station. She was waiting with that irritated look of entitlement on her face. I hadn't planned for this moment, but somehow I found myself speaking up.

"Cecilia, right?"

She turned to me with a look of unpleasant lack of interest, which suggested that the inviting smile from the other day had been my imagination.

"Jack's at the radio station. I think he'll be back in about an hour."

"What the fuck is that?" she said to herself, as if I wasn't there.

"I'm Porter," I continued. "I think we're in the same—"

"I know who you are. Jack talks about you all the time."

I had walked toward her. "Really?" I found myself suddenly unduly excited, which I tried to control.

"I think he must really look up to you or something." She wasn't very interested in this, but stated it as fact.

Without expecting it, I felt like I was blushing, and then worrying that it showed, I became more embarrassed that she would see I was embarrassed, to the point where I must have been bright red.

"Would you like to wait in my room?" I asked Cecilia.

She didn't answer, but she followed me back to my room. She took Jack's usual place on the bed and I sat in the desk chair. She looked put out. She was here for lack of a better option. I watched her, not sure what to say. I felt a drive to grill her in some way, but I was hesitant as to an approach.

"I liked what you said about *Absalom, Absalom!* the other day." I was lying.

"Whatever, it was bullshit. That whole book is bullshit."

"You don't like Faulkner," I said, smirking.

"No. He's a *bad* writer."

"How can you say that? He's a great writer." I was getting aggravated by her presumptuousness.

"'Cause he's boring. It's just crap."

"Just because he's boring to *you* doesn't mean he's a bad writer. Can't you make that distinction?" As I was speaking, I could see my copy of *Absalom, Absalom!* out of the corner of my eye, the bookmark still somewhere in the first thirty pages. The irony of the situation quickly occurred to me; Cecilia had probably read the whole book and closely too, as closely as she was capable of—when she spoke in class, she often referred to the extensive notes that you could see in the margins of her book—and I had barely read any of it, though I was still planning to get to it someday, though we were supposed to be finishing it and starting *Beloved* that same week.

She looked bored by the question and didn't bother replying. But I wasn't satisfied. We had to get to the bottom of this. "Well why even read the book if you don't like it?"

"'Cause I do my work." She seemed to take the question more seriously than I expected.

"But why? If it's all bullshit, why even bother?"

"How the hell should I know. Because I always do my work. It got me in to this school and my parents are paying thirty thousand dollars a year."

Thirty thousand a year was nothing to her parents, I could tell. "But you don't have to go to college. There are other options."

Maybe she was playacting, but she looked at me like this was the first time she had considered this. "Like what?"

"Well, what interests you?" I said, with mild scorn.

She shifted on the bed a little. She still looked pissed off, but why was she even putting up with this? I kept expecting her to ask why I was asking all these questions or to just get up and leave. "I have no idea."

"You don't know what interests you?"

"How the hell should I know. I keep myself busy. I don't think about this kind of crap." I could tell I could easily lose her, but it pleased me that she actually seemed troubled by my questions. To keep her here, I had to ask her something she didn't find boring.

"You like Jack?"

"So? Jack's all right. He's a bit of a loser."

"But he must interest you. You come to his room nearly every day."

"Whatever. He's in love with me."

"How can you tell?"

"'Cause I can tell. And he says so."

"But you must be attracted to him."

"Yeah, so? I like Jack. I said that."

"Well, why do you think he's in love with you?"

"I said, I can tell—"

"No, that's not what I mean. Why is he in love with you? I mean what about you made him fall in love with you?"

She was quiet a moment and she arched her back a little, cat-like. Then she just shrugged.

"Does he ever say?"

She hadn't been looking at me, but then she turned toward me. "Do you find me attractive?"

I returned her gaze somewhat uncomfortably. I wondered if she was coming on to me and if I was looking at her as though I were responding to that, perhaps even trying to look seductive. I wanted to turn it off. "No." I turned away. "No, I don't. No offense or anything.

You're just not my type." I was fumbling. "That's why I'm curious what Jack sees in you."

I could feel her still looking at me and her expression seemed not to have changed. "I don't believe you."

"What do you mean you don't believe me?"

"I don't believe that you're not attracted to me."

"That's because you think everyone is attracted to you. You can't accept that there are a lot of people who are not attracted to you. Some who may even find you unattractive."

"No, that's not true. A lot of people aren't attracted to me. I don't like it, but I can tell when they aren't."

I looked over at her, but not at her face—at her enormous chest, the cleavage showing under her V-necked sweater. I couldn't help it. Then I found myself getting out of my chair and moving toward her. I sat for a moment on the side of the bed and hesitated. She just looked at me a little bemused. I had already started to make a move and I had to follow through with it. I started leaning into her and then felt the force of her hand on my shoulder. She was smiling. It was a horrible smile. She got up and went for the door. "Tell Jack I'm looking for him."

"Wait." I was in a panic. "But you were . . . You were coming on to me." I said it as if I demanded confirmation.

She stood in the crack of the door and shook her head. "No, *you* were coming on to *me*. I'm not attracted to you." And then the killer: "You and I can just be friends, Porter." It was a totally ridiculous thing to say, given the circumstances. Had she said it with a smirk to be nasty, I wouldn't have hated her so. Or even if she had said it just as a reflex, like it was something you say at such a moment, even if she were slightly aware it wasn't really appropriate, then it wouldn't have been so bad. But she said it ingenuously, as if it were somehow a real concession on her part, made all the worse by the little touch of using my name.

"But I'm not attracted to you either," I weakly protested. It should have been worth a laugh on her part, but if she was even listening, she didn't acknowledge it, and closed the door behind her.

The next day Jack didn't come to my room. I worried that Cecilia had told him what had happened and now he somehow thought less of me. I wanted him to come so I could know what she said. In some ways just to confirm what happened. I went through the previous evening in a series of permutations. I alternated moments of extreme shame with a revisionist theory: I tried to tell myself that she had been coming on to me, but had rejected me just to spite me, to make me more attracted to her. And I felt satisfaction in the idea that it hadn't worked. She had blown her one chance with me. In a moment of weakness, I had come on to her, and rather than seizing the moment, she had blown it and now she was the one who would suffer.

Mid-afternoon the following day there was a knock at my door. I got up to answer it with trepidation, expecting Jack, but when I opened the door, there stood Cecilia. I felt a secret satisfaction. She had come back out of compulsion.

I played it cool. "Cecilia? " I smirked. "I thought since I had sufficiently offended you I wouldn't have the pleasure of seeing you again."

"Jack's not in his room. So I thought I would stop by yours and wait. That is, if you don't attack me." She smiled.

I let her in the room and she sat down on the bed. I went back to the desk chair. I couldn't help but ask, "Did you tell Jack what happened?"

She could tell I was anxious for the answer and so she looked at me silently for a while before speaking. "No." She seemed as if she was going to say more, but didn't. I felt ill at ease.

"Why not?"

Again she waited and then said, "I thought, why should I fuck up your friendship?"

"Well, since you didn't like me attacking you, why did you come back here? Did you like me asking you a lot of questions?"

She laughed a little. It was the first time I had seen her laugh. "No, I didn't like that much either. But I guess I find you sort of interesting."

"Is that a compliment?"

"If you like." She smiled almost sweetly. Why was she being so friendly?

Neither of us said anything for a moment. I was trying to think of something to say, but then she hesitated for moment and spoke. Her tone had become distant. "I was thinking about what you said. About how I don't know what interests me."

"I didn't say that. I think you did."

"Well, whatever." She wasn't smiling anymore. "I just, I think it's true."

She wasn't looking at me. It was as if she had just made a confession. I wasn't really sure what I was supposed to say. I was about to rise and go over to her, to comfort her, but thought better of it.

"Well, I think that's normal, you know, at our age, to not necessarily know what we want." My voice sounded hollow, forced. I wished I could erase everything I was saying. "I mean, even I—" I stopped. Even I, what? What did I know? The words just stopped, she was barely listening to me, and so there was no reason to go on.

"I better go." She got up and left without looking at me and I didn't do anything to stop her.

After she was gone, I cursed myself for not keeping her there. I couldn't tell if I was elated or depressed. I paced around the room thinking about our conversation. Clearly, I offered something to her. I had hit upon something about her that no one else had, something she didn't want to face. And she had come back to me to find some sort of solution. But I had left her hanging. I had let her know that there was nothing I could do for her.

I didn't hear from Cecilia or Jack for the next couple days, but I found myself thinking about Cecilia constantly. And well, it gets kind of embarrassing, but I was more than just thinking about her—I was fantasizing about her. The fantasy involved that image I had of her in her towel. That come-hither smile was usually followed by an unfastening of the towel, an unveiling of those breasts. And it just ended there, just trying to imagine that chest, and I'd lie down on my back on the bed in the dark, covered from head to foot with blankets, and stroke myself. There she was, the towel rising up in front, then the unfastening of it, and then I'd try with all my powers to conjure up an image of that enormous chest laid bare for my gaze, but the image was always out of focus. Sometimes, I tried to transplant images of breasts I had seen before onto Cecilia's chest, but usually it turned into huge perfectly round fake breasts awkwardly grafted onto her frame like some sloppy Photoshop fake nude slowly downloading on the Internet. I'd continue to stroke myself trying to revisualize the unfastening of the towel, and this would repeat itself until finally, though never fully satisfied, I could no longer contain myself, and would spurt out over my hand onto the sheets.

Don't think I take any pleasure in writing about this. The mode here is compulsive confession. If I could write about anything else I would. And while I'm at the confession stuff, it may sound weird, but this was the first time I had ever been able to masturbate. I mean I had had sexual fantasies before, I had looked at sexual pictures and videos and found myself getting aroused, but I had never completed what I had started. I had never discovered the ritual of jerking off— so advertised as a rite of passage for pubescent boys. There just always seemed something sort of sad about it. All the boys doing it and talking about it afterward. I had always felt that I hadn't done it when I was thirteen and I hadn't done it when I was fifteen, so why start now? My time had come and gone. But it was the repulsive image of Cecilia that made me discover masturbation about eight years too late. The repulsive and beautiful but always unfinished image of Cecilia.

I looked for Cecilia in our Modern American Novel lecture, but didn't see her. It was a big class so it wasn't impossible that I had just missed her. Impatiently I anticipated our Friday section. Surely I would confront her there, probably after class. Go up to her, I wouldn't need to say much, but she would understand. Perhaps we'd get some lunch or something after section. The tricky thing, of course, would be avoiding Jack. I wouldn't want him to see me talking to her, but since they rarely left together after section, and since Jack and I never spoke to each other after section, it would still be a delicate operation but there was probably some way I could finagle it. And so what if Jack did see us? What was really so wrong if Cecilia and I had developed a friendship. I decided finally that I wanted Jack to see Cecelia and me together.

Friday arrived and Cecilia did not show up to section. Jack, of course, was there as usual. Without Cecilia the section felt exceptionally empty and endless. I realized how much I had relied on my annoyance with Cecilia to entertain me during section. I went up to Jack after class.

"Hey."

"Hey."

"What's up?

"Not much."

We walked for a while, heading in the direction of our dorm. Jack hadn't come by my room in nearly a week and I thought of asking about this, but I didn't. Instead I asked about Cecilia. "What's up with you and that girl?"

"Which girl?"

"You know, Cecilia. The one from our class."

"Oh, her. Yeah, she's kind of nuts."

"Are you guys still seeing each other?"

"We were never really seeing each other. It was just, you know. Anyway, she went home."

"What do you mean 'went home'?"

"She went back with her parents to Texas. She gets these migraine headaches. And she got a real bad one last week and had to be hospitalized. And then her parents came and picked her up. She got incompletes in her classes and she went back to San Antonio. I don't know. She's really fucked up. I guess she's hoping to come back for next semester, but we haven't spoken since she left. There's a lot of baggage there that I'm not interested in getting involved in."

I was in shock. I could feel my heart beating rapidly and my face getting flushed. Jack didn't seem to notice, or if he did, he respectfully ignored it, but he wasn't really the perceptive type. We walked in silence for a while. Finally Jack spoke. "She told me you tried to kiss her."

Did he mean to suggest that this had contributed to her migraine? I wondered what else she had told him about me. I didn't say anything. Finally Jack spoke again. "Don't worry. I'm not pissed at you or anything."

"It was stupid of me," I muttered.

"Really, I don't care. I was just a little surprised. You didn't seem too fond of her. Anyway, she was a real weirdo. A good screw, but a weirdo." A pause and then, "And amazing tits."

We were walking. I was walking and Jack was walking beside me. It was okay, I thought to myself. Everything was fine. But why was I thinking these things? Why did I need to think "Everything is fine"? Was it because of Cecilia? Was I upset that Cecilia was having problems? Did I feel responsible? Or was I upset that I might never see her again? Did I feel that Cecilia's happiness was dependent on me or that mine might be dependent on her? Both ideas seemed so ridiculous that I forced myself to smile. Have you ever forced a smile for no one's benefit but your own? It's a weird feeling. And weird is not an adequate word. It's something more or less than a feeling.

"Jack, do you ever feel that . . ." I was almost mumbling. I was walking. Everything was fine. No need to talk, but this was a desperate moment, perhaps I could reach out, say the right thing. "Do you . . . Do you ever feel like you're . . . fading?"

"Are you all right? What are you talking about?" Was he concerned or just annoyed? I couldn't tell. I should just get away without anything seeming too weird. I should just get away and walk around by myself. Everything was fine.

"I don't know. Nothing. I was just thinking about something. I remembered I have to . . . I'll see you later." I took a left turn and Jack may have muttered "See ya," or something to that effect, I'm not even sure, and I'm not even sure if what I just said I had said was really what I had said, I hoped it was that coherent. I just got away from him and felt something like relief when I did. Without thinking about it, I started heading toward the Main Green. It was an unseasonably nice day. Not warm exactly, but clear sky, warm for the East Coast in November, maybe fifty degrees—the kind of day that makes people say, "What a nice day." I started thinking about my short-term future—things I had to do, reading for class, papers, enjoying, appreciating this nice day. I was forcing myself of think about this stuff, to think practically about the real world. Private liberal arts college, they say, is not the real world. But it really is, only for everyone else, not for me, for whom there is no real world. I was thinking to myself, I should make a plan. I had things to do, the plan could be made for me. Another few weeks left of the semester, finals, and then back home to my parents' house for five weeks, winter break. And then back here and then another semester and then another year and I graduate and what then? The Main Green was crowded, people on their way to or from class, people just milling about, people relaxing on the stairs of Roosevelt Hall, on a day in which, if you were most anyone but me, you would run into someone you knew and make some idle or genuine promise to call him or her or maybe decide to go get a cup of coffee right then and there. "That's too funny!" I heard someone say. And then "Oh, fuck off!" but playfully, accompanied by laughter.

I'm leaving something out that's hard to explain. My panic was too vague, without insight. It was just weakness. It would have been some consolation if I had known that I could have claimed to be having a nervous breakdown, but as a therapist I saw months later told me, it sounded like I thought I was going to have a nervous breakdown, but didn't. Even my nervous breakdown was only in my head. I thought about calling Cecilia, and in fact that's how I now imagine the story should end: a phone call in which I let her know in just the right way felt for her, that I was willing to relinquish all my defenses and be there for her if she felt she needed me. And for her part, well, no, I can't really imagine how the dialogue would go, but she would let me know that while there was nothing I could really do, she appreciated my call, and that in some way I had already done enough. There would be no declaration of love, I can't even fantasize that, just a moment of barely articulated but implicit understanding that would give this story a conveniently bittersweet closure.

But as it was, I never called Cecilia. Did she come back the following semester? I have no idea because I didn't.

I made it through the semester, passed, barely, my finals. The dissipation of my friendship with Jack was as inconclusive as our friendship itself had been. He slowly stopped coming by my room—we did after all have tests to study for—and for me this was a relief. I kept even more to myself for those remaining weeks, if that's possible, studying or thinking about studying; it's a blur. And then, being back in my parents' house in the room I grew up in for that five-week winter break proved too painfully comforting to escape from—the security of my old insecurities. And my mother told me that if her baby was going to be unhappy, he should stay close by, and my father didn't seem to mind, or maybe notice, that I didn't return to school, or at least my mother's doting on me gave him some respite and perhaps that was all that mattered. But that's another story.

Really, if it only weren't for my little sister. The way I heard her say "That's my brother" in that don't-ask-I'll-explain-later voice to her adorable ponytailed friend with the big eyes as they pass by the TV room where I am flipping channels. How did she suddenly get so pretty and confident? I can feel her leaving me behind. She's the only real witness here, but I'm not worried about the effect I'll have on her. She's perfect enough to feel genuine pity but not enough to lose sleep over it.

Since arriving home, I've had an important revelation: I am depressed. Far from being an upsetting thought, it's something like an inspiration. A thought so obvious that it had never occurred to me—it offers me a context and a cause. I've read the literature of other people having similar revelation: from the self-help bestsellers which perhaps I didn't always read in full—but read enough to know that the authors were writing about was what I am feeling, if not in the way I would write about it or feel it—to the more literary ventures that seem to elevate the stature of my condition. Or should I say, "our condition," because we are all really depressed. Even the apparently happy ones. In fact, they have it worst of all, burying the depression so deeply inside that it fails to express itself at all; the deep internal damage must be monstrous.

At least this got me reading again, which I had been unable to do at school. There were the magazine articles about a national crisis—one out of every four they say—and miracle cures—prescription drugs, regular exercise, a change of diet—quitting coffee, no carbohydrates, more sunlight, whatever . . . I wasn't interested in cures themselves, but the idea of cures—they were out there and some day I would make a plan and follow up on one of them.

To be part of this mass was comforting for a time, but soon I discovered the even more appealing idea that depression is not this common problem which I share with a great portion of the globe, but is instead a problem for the more complicated few. I found myself in pretty good company—Van Gogh, Kafka, Nietzsche . . . an artist's disease. Depression is the natural result of a malaise that wasn't mine, but it was all around us, and I was one of the privileged ones to experience it.

Which brings me to my theory—which explains why I am depressed, and incidentally why maybe Franz Kafka was also depressed, but believe me, were Kafka in this room right now, I'd know enough to spare him my theories. The only way an honest man can escape this vile world is to renounce desire, to see through the façades of pleasure. Which is why I took classes I had no interest in, and why I made no friends—because interest was a false consolation. Interest always involved a ruse and an eventual broken promise. I was no sucker—I was going to be interested in what I chose, not what offered pleasure. I had followed through on my plan. I had in fact been disciplined enough to eliminate the lures of fun, of good times, of desire.

But there's a catch. By renouncing desire I had lost interest in everything and the rather debilitating result was that reality itself had started to lose its reality. For a period of time, after that first episode when I was walking with Jack, I felt myself in some perpetually distracted haze that left me either anxious or tired. Far from being able to celebrate accomplishing my plan of working hard, I found myself hungering for anything that could keep my interest even in the simplest or crudest way—from organizing my old room or my CD collection to looking at amateur porn on the Internet (but no more masturbation mind you, just looking, then turning it off and no thought of Cecilia, not really, rarely) to playing computer video games. At my worst, everything I would do, I would say to myself, *I am doing this now.* "I am brushing my teeth now," I would think to myself while brushing my teeth. "After I brush my teeth, I'll walk back to my room and get in bed." Depression, I decided, is a victory experienced as a loss.

And so I granted myself an interest. I allowed myself to be interested in the phenomenon of depression itself. And to some extent, it worked. I was able to focus on the subject of depression and this made me less depressed. But it felt in some way to be a temporary solution. The goal consciously was to kick the ladder away once I had climbed it—to use my newfound focus to perhaps go back to my original plan of devoting myself to intellectual work, or at least to get to the point where I could get distracted by a TV sitcom, and not simply focus on this depression business. The idea of depression was only fascinating to me as a discovery. Once it became a routine, I knew it would only make me depressed.

It's now summer and I'm going to start at a not as reputable local school in the fall. I'll probably even live in a dorm, not at home, but we'll see, I'm still trying to figure that one out. I've now decided that I'll only take classes that are immediately appealing to me. I don't have to be interested in science or history. It's okay if I can't do everything, I should at least be able to do something. At this point, I should name that thing that I've found I can do or really like doing. Maybe I'm really some sort of math genius, or maybe I'll take up painting. Really, I'm more concerned about you than I am about myself. I'm fine. I'm all right being at home and watching TV and I could care less what my sister thinks. But for you, I should at least be able to offer some better form of compensatory closure than just that I'm going back to school. But really I just can't come up with anything, not right now.

Snake, World Drawings

Louise Belcourt

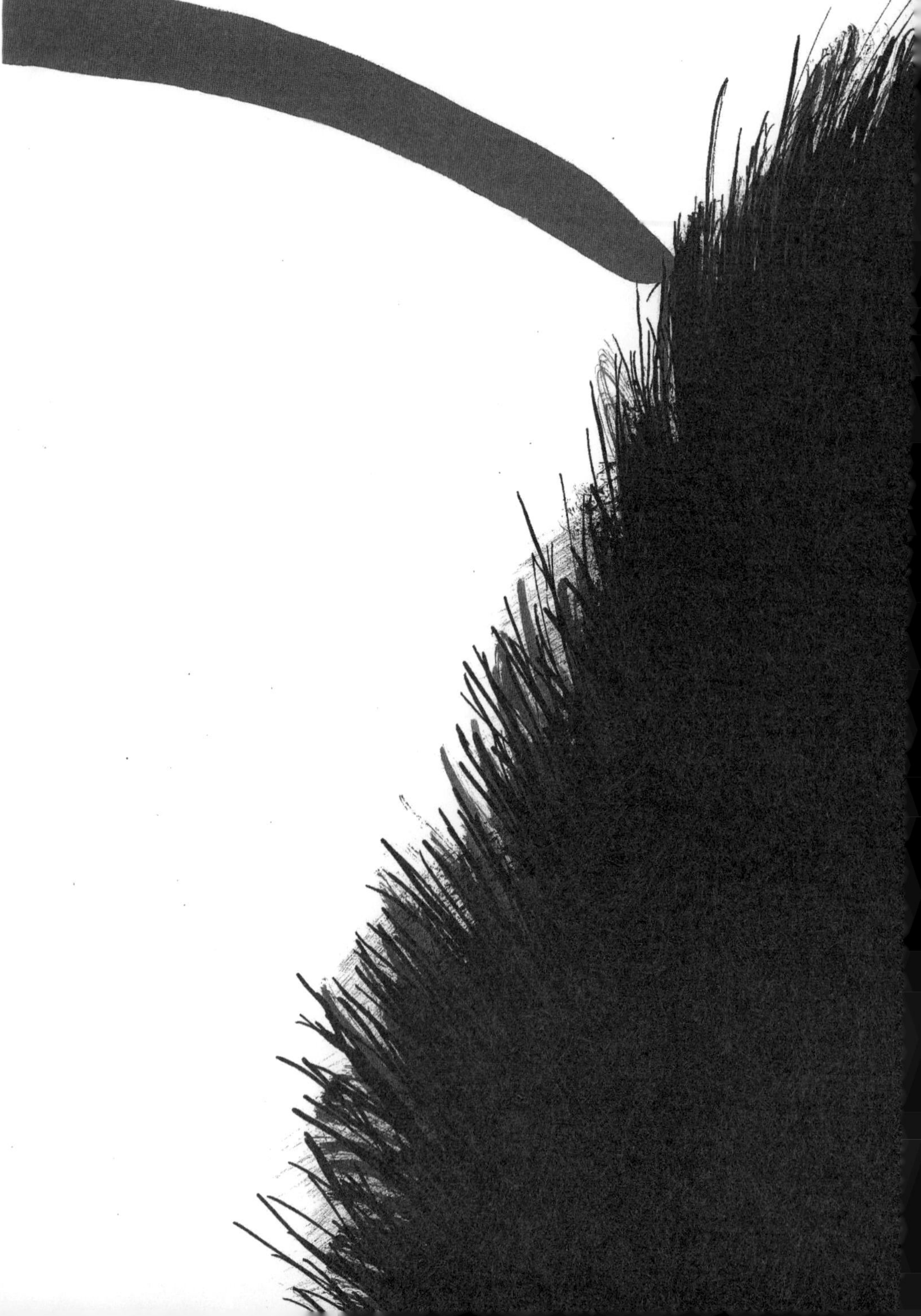

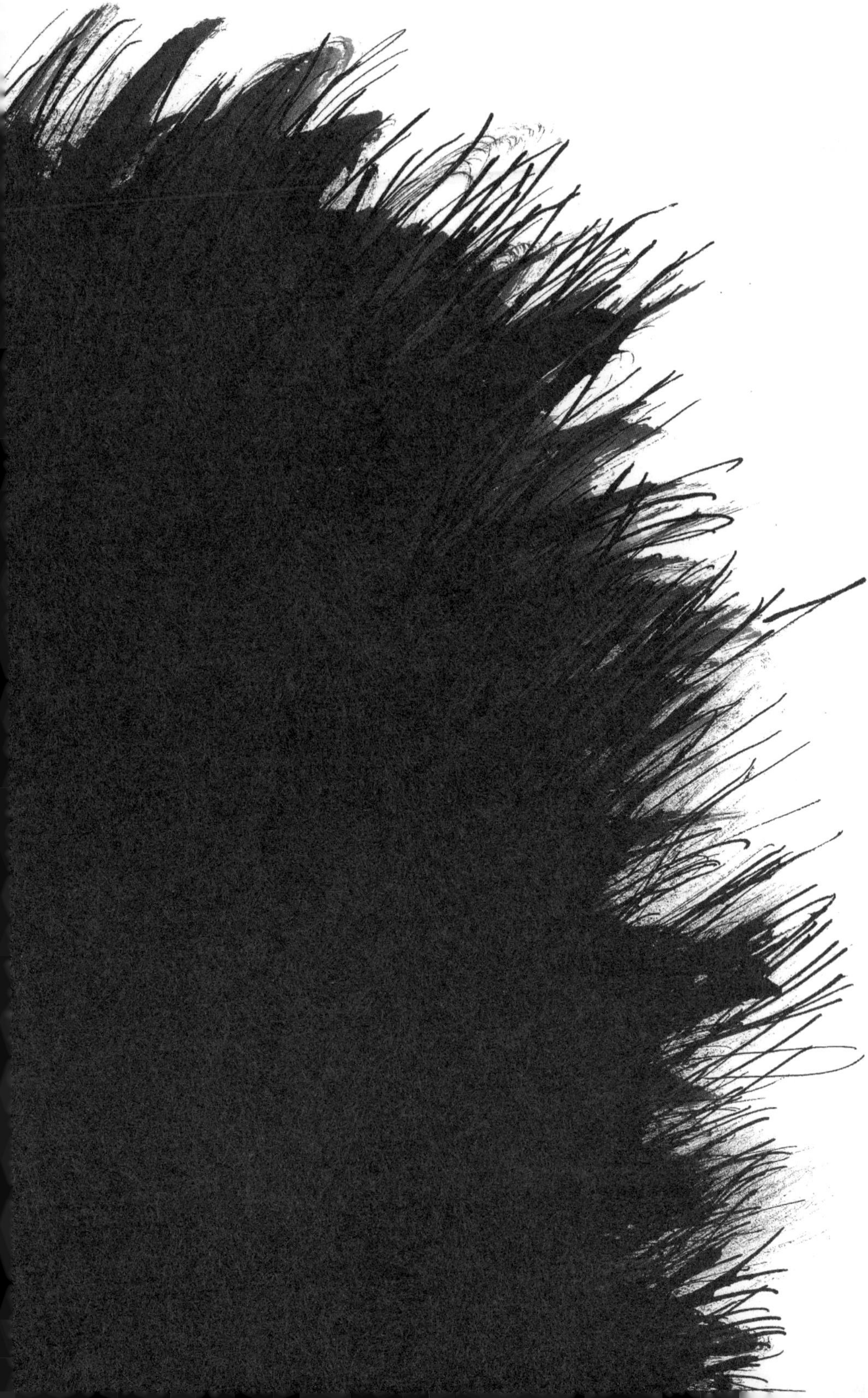

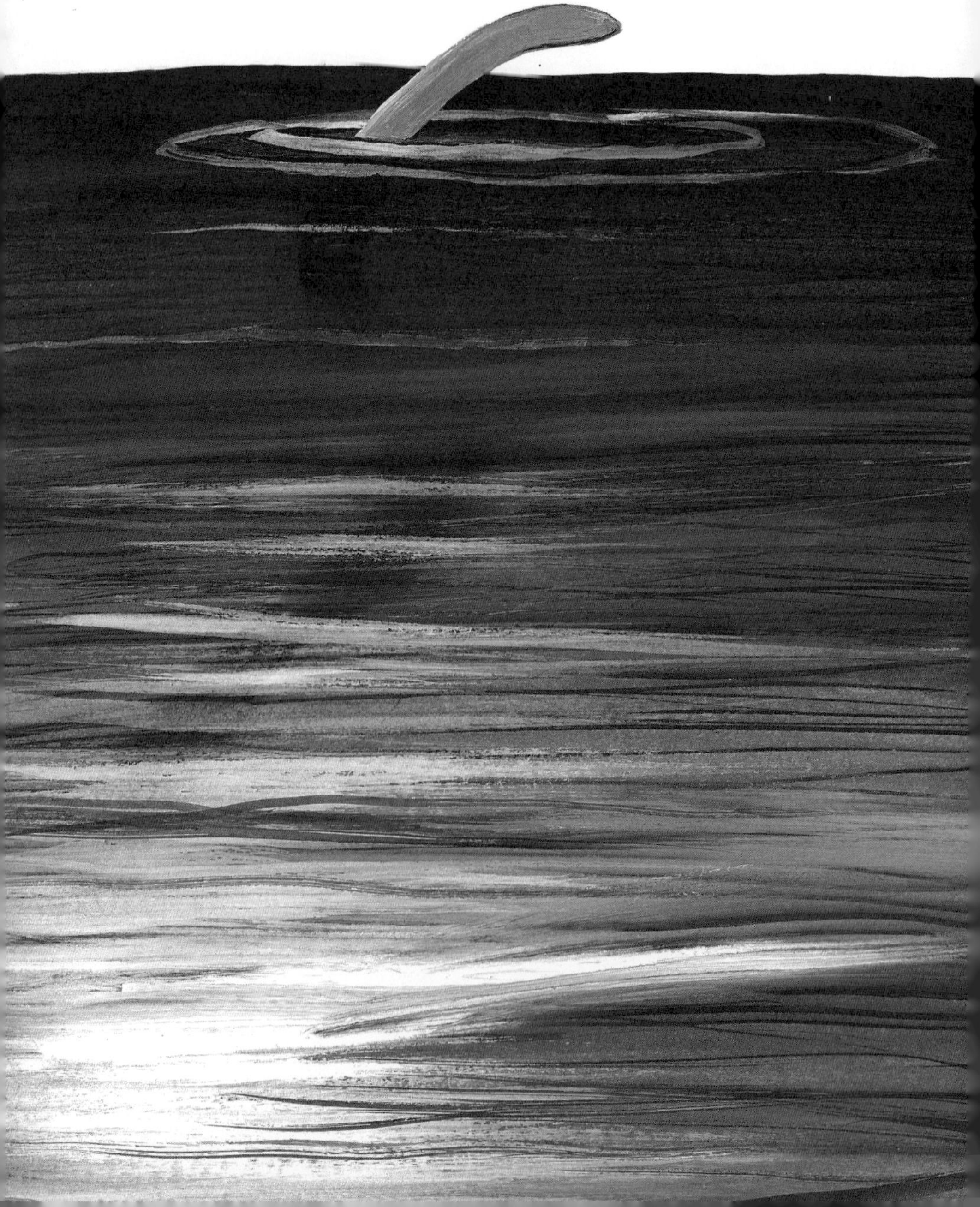

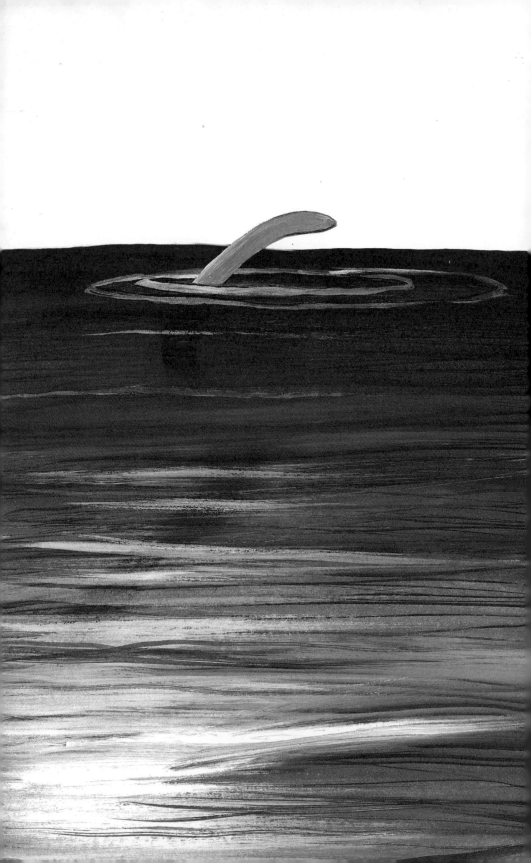

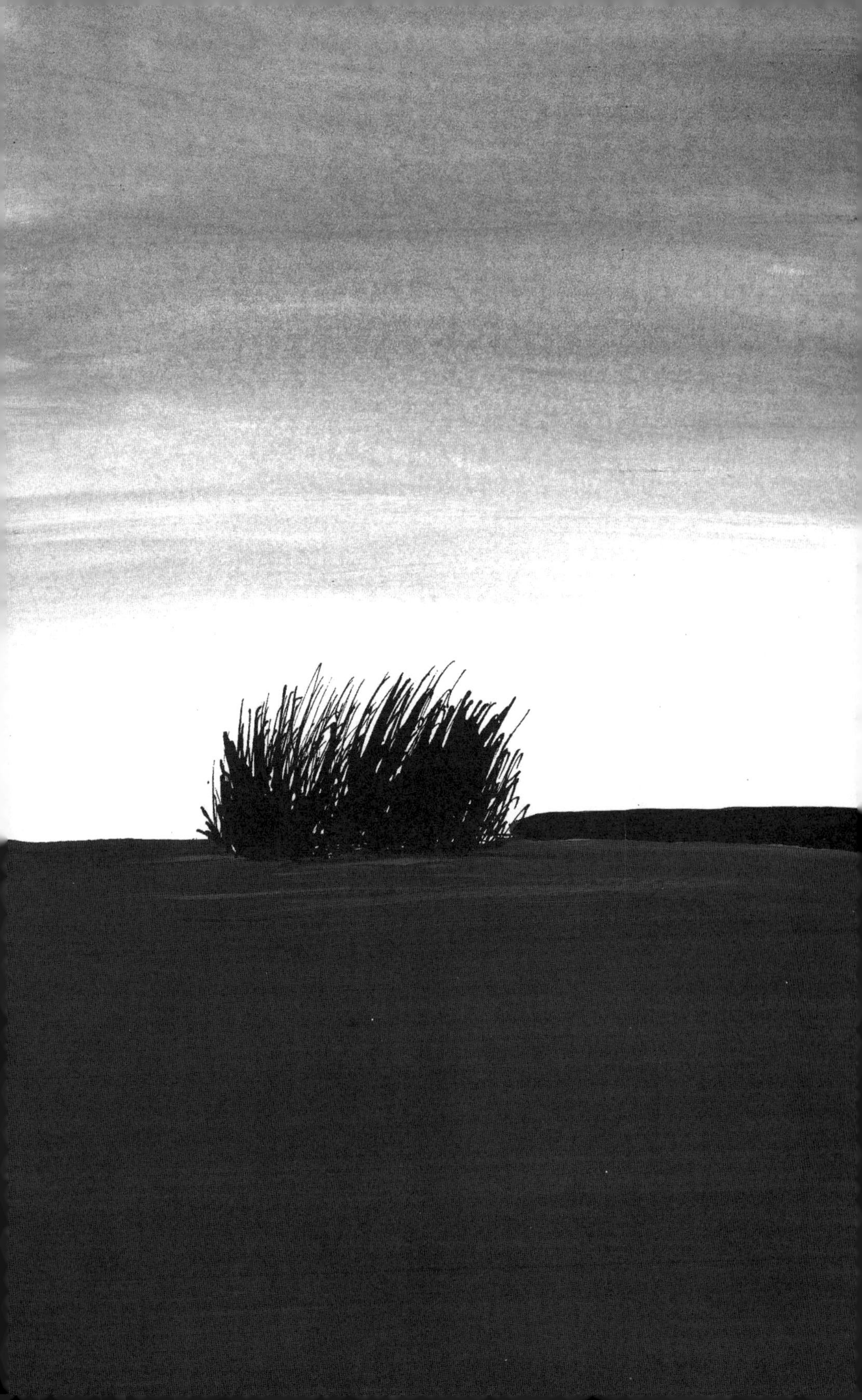

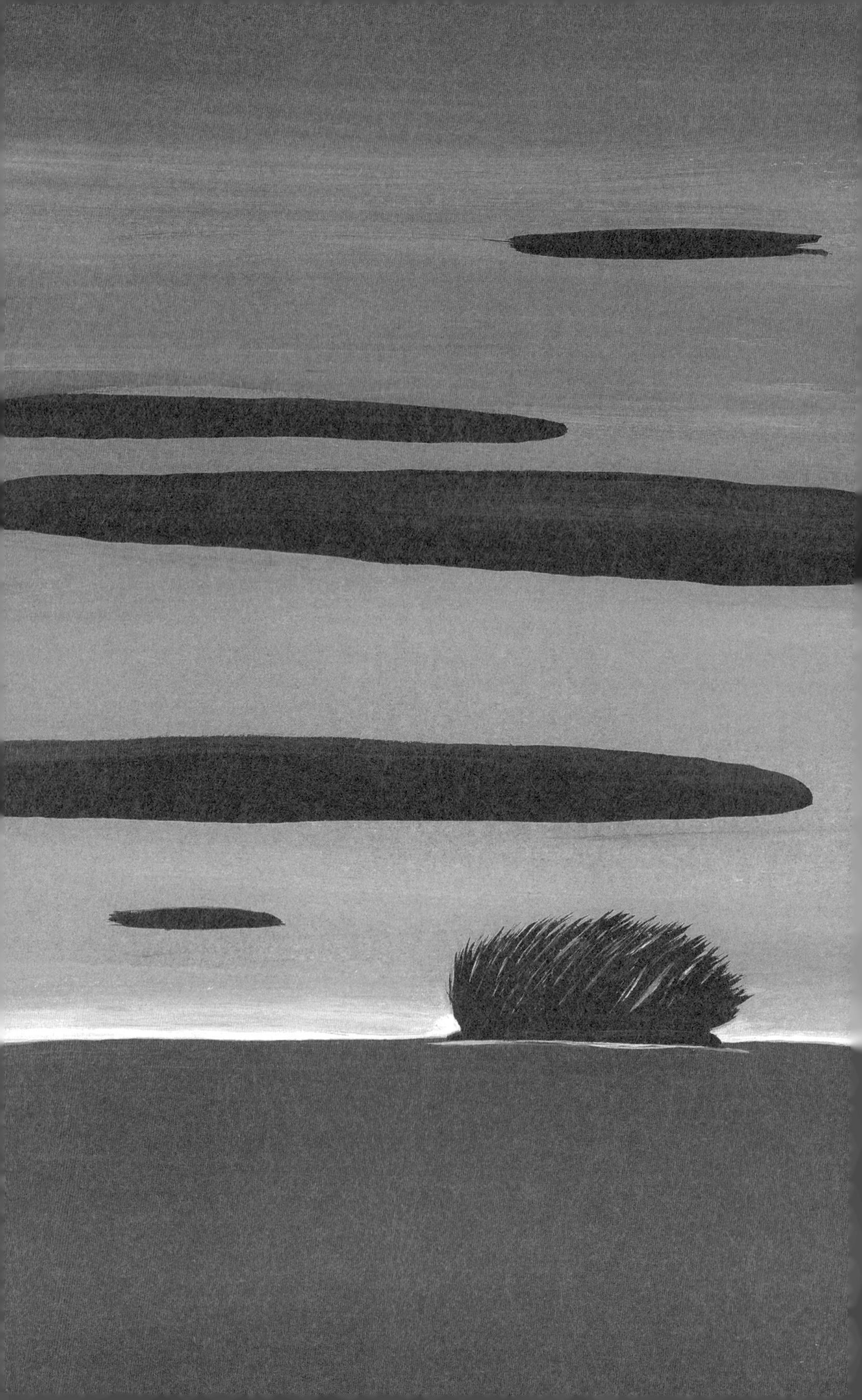

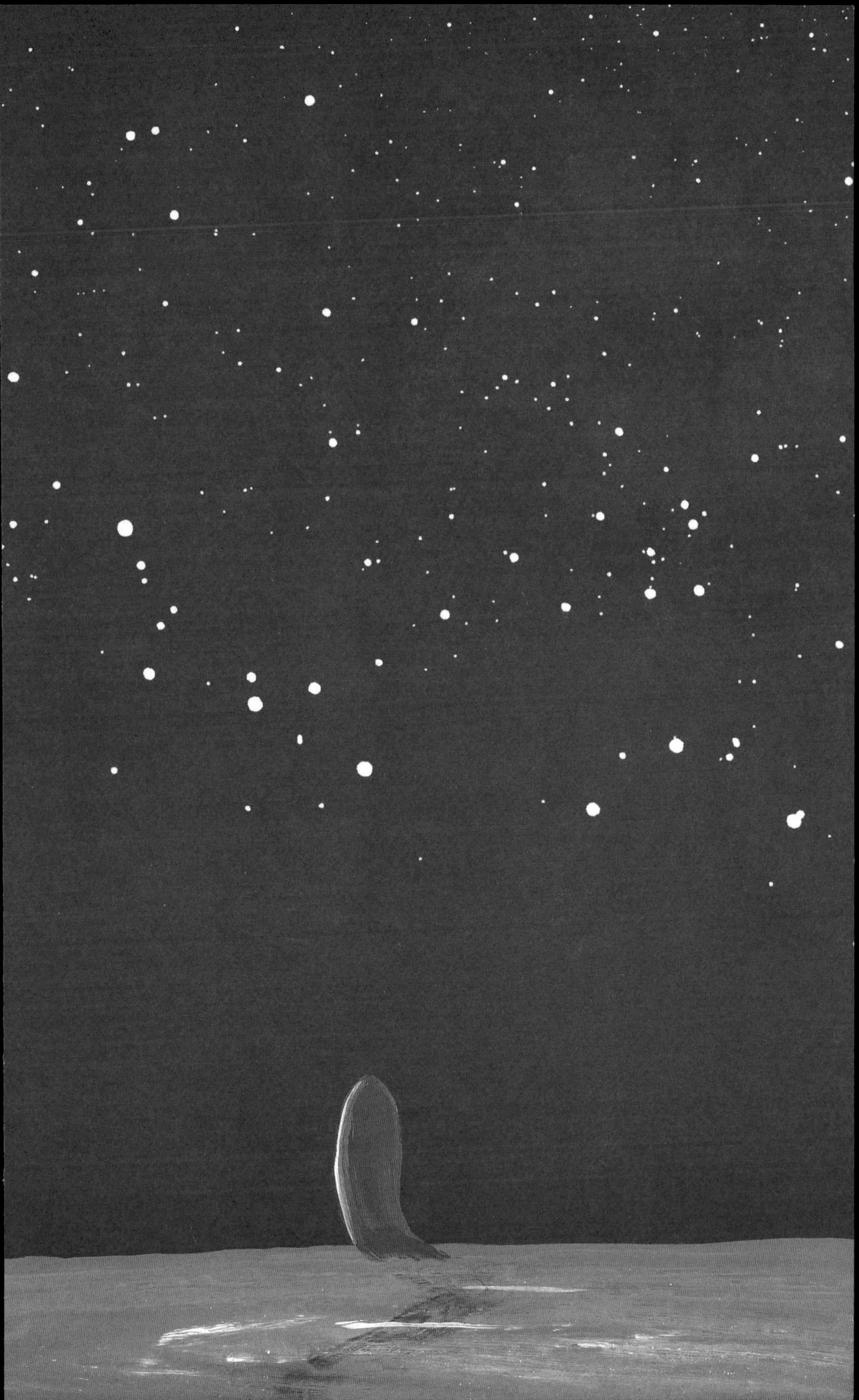

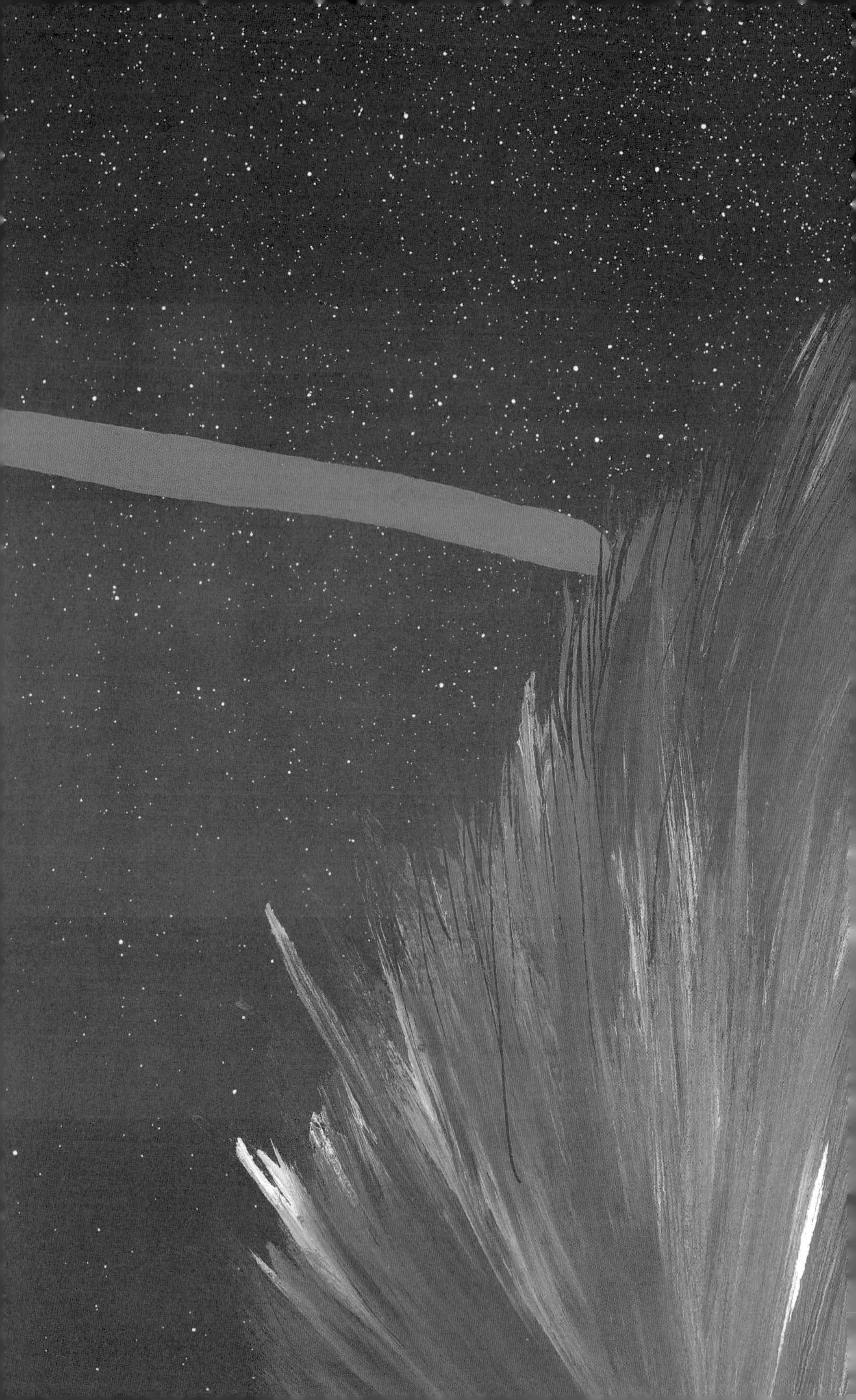

"My parents don't love the American dream," Anya says, tossing the day's mail into the recycling bag that hangs by her sink. "They love the Soviet dream, which is to be in America drinking better quality vodka than they get in Odessa." (Grove, page 97)

Time for the Flat-Headed Man

Noy Holland

IT'S COME TO ME TO INTRODUCE TONIGHT'S READER.

My wife asked would I. She says it's easy, easier for you, you do it easily. She makes it difficult—to stand here, to open her mouth, it's a struggle, she says. I said, Yes, dear.

Yes hello, dear.

I'm not ungrateful.

It clears my head some—to stand up here and talk to you in a grown-up sort of way.

We have, as you know, the two children. The girl, a boy. They are thinking she is going to get better, our girl. Give her time, they say, some months to grow—

Yes, come in, come in. I'm glad you made it, every one of you. Blinking into the snow.

I was talking about our children. The girl, a boy.

I taught our boy to ride his bike. That was nice. He skids out, lays a patch, wants to show me. Shows everybody his scabs. Lookit look: a scab on every joint he can get to. Point of pride.

He says, "Our baby's name is Noodle and I like to suck her hair."

And so he does, I let him, no harm in that. He sets his lips around the hole in her headbone, slurps in a satiny frill. I think she likes it.

How nice to see you. You few I know. You look lovely, really you do. Hello, darling up there. I like your muffler. I like your hats and shoes.

She missed the winters, my wife, it's why we came here. She missed all the different clothes—the heavy coats, the bundling up. You could pass your long life in a halter top in the town we came north to get out of. The air velvet. Squinch owls and duckweed, pickled eggs. A pontoon boat with the radio on, making laps on the side-by lake.

Our boy was small there, he was a baby. You could sit him in his bucket on the lakeside in the sun. We had egrets. Once a wood stork. Peahens on the roof of the cabin—tatting at the nailheads, the pipe coming up. Anything bright they could get to.

She comes from Akron, tonight's reader. Akron by way of Toledo. By way of Mayor's Income. That's in Tennessee.

She writes poems. This is my introduction. Wrote a book of stories, skinny thing, lot of white on the page. She's got two kids same as our two kids. A good gig in Tuscaloosa. A hottie in the chute, have a look at her, some lanky buckaroo. It's what I've heard.

You ever hear of the ones they break the bones on the young to get them set back right?

And it works!

While they're small. Little miracles. Such a miraculous day and age with all they know and do.

Our boy said, "Papa."

We were lying in bed and he was messing with himself, his little package, trying to make the hole bigger he said. "Papa, look." He stretched it up to show me. "Doesn't it look good?"

His *woowoo*, he used to call it.

"In a few days your woowoo will bloom into a thousand flowers."

He's got the skin on still and he forces it back and out comes this purple ball. It looks all wrong, it looks rotted.

He says, "When you die I hope you're a frog and I will catch you and I will keep you in my bucket."

I liked to think of him there in the heat where we lived rounding up snakes and frogs, growing up, fishing. Little barebacked nut-brown boy. Swinging through the trees on a strangler fig. I liked thinking of him being a man there sitting on an overturned bucket.

He'd have a pontoon boat. He could think there. He'd have a radio, a little old crackly transistor of the sort that will hang in your shirtfront pocket. A gentle man. A party of one, making his pointy rounds.

A simpler life.

Of course we're lucky.

Even the baby—couldn't she be lucky?

She's not old enough, the baby, you can't break them yet, her little buttery bones. So we keep her stuffed into her harness. Keep our chins up. As per. We think in pictures. It's a help.

She wags her arms a bit, but otherwise—

I'll just say it. I'm not cut out for it, we're not.

We're cut to gather. Gather and hunt and think—I used to think, have a thought through in my chair. My chair! Pretty thing. Shoved into the corner of my room.

I lay the girl down at the back of the house, pull the door to, steal away. Have a sit.

She has to lie there. She's just little, little bunch, just a nugget. I could drop her through the mouth of the woodstove, be done with her in a day.

Who am I?

Because who am I really, do you think, to her?

She's just little. She doesn't know me. Give her time, time enough, some months to grow, she'll point me out, say, "Bapa."

The ennobling moment.

The blow to the head. Then the knees go.

Like the heartbeat, first time, the first picture, her little face full on through the tissue, the fiber and brine, and she waved. Here I come, she seemed to say, don't try to stop me.

You do what you have to do. Burn through. Drop into my hands, big Papa's hands, and he flinches, woozy, I was blinking out.

They say it's easy, it is all she knows: harness, plaster, spreading bar. Bapa. Hot. Brother. Dog. All the little cups and pulleys.

Her brother drew on her face with a crayon, drew a face.

I was elsewhere. I was taking my ten deep breaths. As per. You take a breath, keep moving. They can't move, you think you're safe, you think they lie there, okay, and what could come? Well here we come. Bapa. Mama. Brother. Dog.

My wife busts through the door going, "Mama. Come to mama, baby, I'm home."

The old egg clutch. The gladdened hand. She is spitting milk, she is weeping. Bringing the bacon home.

What I like?

I liked lying on the bed on the phone with her, nothing left to say.

I like a good outside shower, looking up through the moss and leaves. Our man in his boat, turning circles. Little lake.

Our lake was shrinking. It was dirtier every year we lived there, the water siphoned off. Lake Rosa. After Rosa. It was storied. All the good stuff—rape and pillage, dirty Feds. Stills in the woods and sink holes you could drop your murdered through. Gothic excess. I always liked it. I liked the old gin joint sloughing on the banks. The desolated piers. Our boy was small there. Sit him on the slope in his bucket in the sun and the peahens would stroll down and gawk at him.

Then the rumors flared up. Something had killed a peahen, a fellow was missing his dogs. Two, and then another, and then somebody else, and pretty soon they had got a posse up and were combing the lake for gators. They came upon an ancient bull in the muck, bellowing and sluggish, and everybody had a go at him, and beat him on the head with pipes. They opened him up and, looky-loo, found a dewclaw, hair balls, gizzards. A broken chain of vertabrae, a clutch of radio collars.

A boy bloodied to his elbows, weeping.

The pontoon boat run aground.

I'd say I liked that. The freakish tableau.

The penny in your pocket mildewed.

"Penny?" says my wife.

Nothing to report. A polar cold. The wind chirrups.

Cheer up. Cheer up.

Sugar girl? Forgot your hat! Now get. Safe home. Look both ways twice. Don't let the door hitcha in—

Somebody else? In a hurry? Scooting out?

Nice to stand here. Talk to big folks.

Poems and stories, she does both, she does the colonies, the clusterfucks, lunch at the door, a little basket. Qi gong, feng shui, reps at the gym. Have a look at her. Stringy thing, she used to dance, flattened abs, the haunch on her, quite the hottie. But you can smell it on her: she's a mother. She's submerged.

Sniff her out, use your nose: she will have turned some. She'll have soured, that's a hint. Something's ferny. Grown in, they're grown over. Earthen, a flicker: then gone. You can't reach them. You can't console them. You touch them and they sink away.

What's to do?

I sweep the floors clean. I make the meals.

The boy sprints at her. The baby wakes and cries.

The ravaged female. Our Lady of the Mount. Miss DMV.

Fresh from the stirrups. As if.

Spun up—a little ball, a webby mass. Maybe she moves some, you try to move her. "Hey?"

But no it's nothing, she insists. It's just she's tired.

I'll give you tired, what the fuck. I'll give you nothing.

Sit down, sit down. You think I'm finished?

"I amn't finished," says our boy.

We'll make a night of it—the wide belts, the tools. The wonder, the stunt.

She's got her papers out, the dog-eared book. She'll get up here, find her page. Proclaim the miracle. Another living body in her living body yada yada yada yada nothing but give give give.

YOU SIT.

Let a man have a little fun, why not? Air his mind some. I amn't finished.

"I amn't going to hit you," our boy says. "I amn't going to kiss you. I amn't going to get a sword and chop you in two."

"Into what?" I ask.

"A zillion pieces."

My mother's dead now. Which makes life simpler. It's not a joke, it's true.

When my old man was away, he was away quite a bit, I used to go to my mother in her bed. I never asked could I. We never spoke of it. She wore a nightgown the planets were pictured on and I knew in the morning when my father was away that she would lie in bed and let me pick at the sleeve at the small gray beads of cloth I came to keep with the hair from her pillow I found and the skiff of foam kneaded to dust that I tapped from the toes of her slippers. I lay in the dark in the bedheat in the wet bready smell of her, not moving, pretending to sleep, I was a boy, and then not, too old for it, mommy's boy, and disgusted, and in my disgust it grew easier for me to picture my mother in stirrups, strapped in, laboring, gassed, while the waxy molten globe of my head burned through her.

I never touched her: if I touched her she would burst into flames. I lay away from her and felt the seed move in me, heating up, pearly, the flashing tails, the race to the sea. The bliss of sleep enmired.

I would sleep enmired in the puddle I had made, happy and ashamed.

My brother served us waffles each morning and we lay propped up with the TV on and ate them with our hands. I wouldn't speak to her. I wanted to throttle her. I couldn't stand it: to have a mother: to have grown my arms and legs in her, my cock and balls, gill and lung, every plug and socket.

I wanted to come from nothing, from air, a cloud, the heavens jeweled. The tinted distance.

She sweeps in, my wife. Hello, hello. She's a special event, she's a goer.

I report on the daily doings, tell her what she has missed. The shitty baths. The scabs, some stunt. Some funny little peep her baby makes.

I say, "She spent the day on her backside. Lying there hoping to grow."

My wife hovers, *coodle coo*. Then to bed. She's spent. Asleep by the time I get there—dreaming, I guess, of you. Some one of you tamping burning coals deep into her nostrils. You've pulled her teeth out.

And she's a mother!

Full-grown. Pushing forty, my wife.

"Those are longing," says my boy, and he swats at her breasts. It's not a joke, it's true.

What I'd like?

I'd like a day on that fellow's pontoon boat, a radio, the white-hot marvelous sun. I'd lash the helm, keep her circling. Sun on my ass, blister my nose. Sit and drink some. Think a few gothic thoughts through.

We got fathers out there? You a father?

See? He's going, *Yeah. Baby, yeah.* Fucking sit there.

"I mean it," says my boy, "I'm honest. I'm just standing here, I'm honest."

He's at the bedside, the baby howling. His crayons poking out of his pockets.

Sweet doll. Sugar girl.

He'll make it up to her, he'll saw at his trousers with a Lego. He says, "I'm gonna make these littler so when Noodle ever has a baby then her baby can grow into them. Wouldn't that be cool?"

He puts a dress on, very flowery, a lacy thing she's to grow into, should she grow. "And what shall we call you?" I ask him.

He's sitting on the pot, thinking. "I'd like to be Glorious Angel."

And so he is, spinning through the kitchen with his dress lofting up.

And I am Claybrain, Hiccalump, Clumpfoot, Tuk.

A man in need. Could stand a drink. Stand to sit down.

"We lived in Florida?" he asks.

"I was a baby?"

"Yes."

We lived in the land of the halter top. We snived in the snand of the lalter snop. Hip. Pop. Pifflewop.

How nice to see you. You're very tall.

I brought pictures. The boy, a girl. You see they're lovely.

We keep her dress pulled down. You can imagine—the little stir-rups, fresh out, a new girl from the womb. Her feet folded against her shinbone. Stuffed in. She's filleted, looks like, laid open, very clean.

Little clean plump butterflied lamb.

Still the look on her! Such a beauty.

You drut. Get out, get out, don't think you're sneaking. You and your sneaky friends. Life suckers. Up. UP.

"Let's get a knife for ourselves," my boy says, "and run out there and stick them."

Here's a tip, the rest of you. We go to market.

Take the baby when you go to market, boys, take her anywhere there are girls. It's a charm. Look at that! Little buddings. They want to pet her.

I take the baby down to the pool. You get a daddy in the pool they're a swarm, watch me, little humpy strokes, the water frothing, they walk on their hands, be a horsie, swim me where I can't swim.

I do, and they are kicking, they are breathing fast in my ear.

"And we lived beside a lake?" my boy wants to know.

"We lived beside a lake."

He's forgotten. He's down to stories. Suspicions, omissions. A foreign view.

"And my mother took me out in my bucket?"

"And your mother took you out in your bucket."

"And my mother loved me very much?"

"And your mother loved you very much. And you were her prince. Her angel. And she loved you. And you were all she saw or could think of. And she loved you. You said *ngogn ngogn*. And I loved you. Your papa loved you."

"And my mother set me down in my bucket."

Firstborn, boychild, hoyden.

Mama, Papa, Clumpfoot, Tuk. We make mistakes, give us that. We're only human.

Pin her down, cinch her up. Man the fires. Sweep the floors.

They say a year, tops. That's consolation. They say, "It is all she has ever known."

I say she used to breathe underwater. She was gilled, webbed, a rock, a frog. Amphibious. She was larval. Boiled in the heart of a dying star. She knows plenty.

So they forget: what is that?

They know plenty.

He is lava, lightning, Black Bart, bear. He's a worm, torn up, a withered heart. T. Rex and the woods are burning.

That's him in the tub, hollering—hollowing, he calls it, a pirate song: hardee-eye-yay, hoodee-eye-yoo. He's got his face bunched up around his eye patch. He's using his mother's diaphragm for an eye-patch.

"For a boat," he says, "to kill Noodle with. Kill Noodle."

He's got us racing, on the move: marks get set. "You just keep getting faster and faster," I tell him.

He looks up at me—a long look, sweetly, and says, "And you're getting slower and slower, right?"

Little prince, princelet.

The sun moves because he moves. The leaves are turning. He

wears his tassled hat—which makes the wind blow—which sparks a lightning—which fells a tree.

His mother took him out into the trees one day. This was lake-side—heat and strangler fig, every manner of insect living. Great mounds. She can't get past it. Carried him out in his bucket—a boy in the cool of her shadow, a babe in his mother's arms. Let it go, I say. Well it's hard, it's hard. Hand of God, you could say, but she won't say it.

It's come to me to say it.

"You say I have to say I *forgive* you," our boy says.

Forgive me. Shameful of me.

You see she's leaving.

I used to like it—the feeling she was always leaving, that any moment she would pick up and go. I'd hear her drive off, I wouldn't stop her. After a time I would find some picture of her and sit with it in my chair. All true, every word—I would speak to her, as though to her, a grown man, a fool. I could make myself feel very sexy, and wanting, I wanted her, the way she tucked her toes against my ankles when we loved, such a simple act, as small as that—I could summon every foolishness, every hoarded sweetness—the near-blue skin of her ankle, nicked—the seaside, I pictured, the tide-washed shore—dewy and silken and pale, the skin, where the elastic of her sock pulled tight, ribbed, an imprint, the tide recedes, you wake alone in the glare of love. I was undone by it, wished to be, easily, in passing. I rubbed out the print, smoothed it away—would, would, never had: a missed statistic: the incidence of men in their kitchens goading themselves to tears. Sobbing in their rockers.

Come on back, baby. Come home.

It's me!

Your angel, your prince. Dear old bread stick.

They ought to fix that door. We'll all have dreams of it. Hooked shut. Then the stutter and wheeze.

A woman embarked.

Stealing away through the wintry mix, we can't stop her.

Just as well. We'll stay and speak of her.

She wanted sunshine. The very best for her boy, fresh air for her boy. A little sunshine. Ions, photons, vitamin D. Wanted heat. To be limbered and quiet and slowed. Be his mother. His cooling shade, his softness, *come to me,* becalmed. The slow marvels, she would give him, the glistening ant, the lizard's coppery pouch; mirage—puddled silver in our road, the box turtles gliding above. Her wild boy singing in a secret tongue—tongue of wind, of dog.

He'd have collections: feathers, coins, the ribbed skin of snakes. The beak of a bird, a tree frog. A June bug on a thread. The dream of a life she remembered. The owl in the mimosa. The armadillo in a doze—you could smell it beneath the house.

She set him down. For an instant. Buzzing heat, lake light, the drowse. The wag of the brittled palmetto. She moved off. A thinking woman. Thought: sinkhole, felon, dengue, flood. Not likely. But what of the limb, the pebble thrown, the interstellar iceball? She thought of the arc: velocity: mass: the mathematics of the cataclysmic. Perhaps the wood stork. The kid with a stick, the hand of God. The orangutan sprung from the zoo. All that. Still she moves off.

He isn't far, she thinks, she could hear him. She can almost even see him. Should he need her. It's just an instant, just a couple three minutes she needs just to think, she isn't far, really, just to think some, he's in his bucket, rocks a bit but the ground is soft, he may be sleeping, yes, likely, lucky for her, she can think now, counts the minutes—three, four, loses track—and so she milks it, another minute gone, the list in her head, she will turn back, should, he must be sleeping, poor thing, the breeze from the lake, coolish today, the day pleasing, what is left of it, was, you mustn't blame her. She hears an owl in the trees and turns back—spooked—I never liked it, you hear people say they like it—the hoot, the trill—old owlers, out in the cold, a boy at their heels, in the shadows, the great squeaking hinge of their wings. She went back then. Her boy was shrieking. Strapped in. Just a baby. She'd set him down on a mound of fire ants. Like to carry him off, sure you've seen them. Like on the specials? Just the tiniest things but they swarm.

She came running home back through the trees to me, his bucket swinging against her legs.

We got him hosed off. You couldn't touch him. He stuck everyplace you touched him.

Those little blisters everywhere broke open and they ran.

Fire ants, the heat of the day, you see the logic. We got him strapped in. Sedated. Bound for the icy north.

Move along. That'll fix it. Build a rock wall, saw the trees down. Mop and mow. Now you've got her, you've got her, she's gone.

The nights were quiet. Cold already and quiet. Sundown, sunup. Not a bird, not a frog.

He crawled, he ran. He had a birthday. Said, "Papa, I am four almost. And after this I will be six and after that I will be ten and when I become fifteen I'll drive and I will drive so fast and then I will be twenty. Then I will have one leg. Old people only have one leg and then I will be dead, Papa, and you will come and save me. I will be in a pond."

We get out of the car, snow coming down, we're rushing. He says, "Wait, Papa. I want to feel the cold."

It's like a knife at your throat, to love them. It's like gathering leaves in the wind.

We want the world for them both, we're like anyone.

The smell of home, the dog at the foot of the stairs. Your wife asleep, your children. Fire humming in the stove.

Or something else. And else again. We think in pictures. The dream of a life we remember and slept through while we lived.

The velvety air. The way the trees crooked down—how easy he would find it to climb them.

I think of the lake through the trees where we lived, where she lived as a girl, old Angel Oak, the swinging vines, shrimp you could buy on the roadside. Boiled peanuts. Old coot in the steam on the median, his boy fishing the grate at his knees—a string, a hook, a giving stick—happy with that, horsing, we were happy enough to see them.

We could take a week, go see them. Get some sun on our bumpy bottoms, yellow in our hair. Light out.

It's been a winter, don't you say? I would say it. We came out of our house to come down here our car was gone to the roof in snow. Still we managed, we two.

It's a distance. Quite a drive.

She pulls her eyelashes out. We keep our hats on. She pulls her hair out strand by strand.

That's life, I guess, funny workings, not to fret. It's just I'm—

SIT DOWN.

We all have them—little tics and such, how our minds work. Mine.

I'm not an ogre.

Turn's up, I got you.

Give a hand.

You're very kind, you few, our small tribe, it's just us. The last listeners.

A warm welcome. Come on, Amherst.

I give you Akron.

Give up the post.

I'm gone home, going home.

He likes to lie on my back.

You know the specials? We'll watch the specials: the horned; the frilled; the mighty bird-hipped. Ornithomimus. Avimimus. The theropods, the thecodonts. The king tyrant, T. Rex.

Boy his heart really goes.

Allosaurus, staurikosaurus.

Little god, boy heart.

Leipleurodon—what eats sharks.

You ought to hear him.

Yangchuanosaurus, megalosaurus, tarbosaurus bataar.

Velociraptor: the swift.

Troodon: the wounding one.

All the old dead meat-eaters.

Bile

Stephen Graham Jones

WE WERE IN TOWN TO SEE OUR FATHER DIE. IT WAS CIRRHOSIS OF the liver, all those beers I carried him before I got too old to trust out of his sight, reaching into that second shelf. Raymond was there, with two changes of clothes, one of them a borrowed suit, and then Charline and my three nephews, watching me from around her hips, their hair plastered to their skulls. Thomas couldn't make it, or, he probably could, but like Dad, he was out there somewhere making news himself, getting arrested in a doughnut shop for lewd behavior or being questioned for attempted vehicular regicide, a stolen bobtail truck idling in front of the house, small flags screwed into the front fenders to confuse the presidential escort. This time Dad was in the paper just because he was in the background of an ATM security tape, always watching it.

They took him in to question him and he said he was waiting for the money to fall out, which Charline said was reasonable enough, right? Right?

I didn't bring a suit. Maybe I'll wear Dad's if we can ever figure out where he was living. We take turns with it, one of us staying bedside, playing go-between for him and the nurses, who are trying not to get attached, while the other two scour the city hotel by hotel, asking the same question: old Indian guy, short hair, bad skin, one milky eye? Big Plume? By the second day I can pinpoint the exact moment in my question when the clerks stop listening to me, when I become one voice of many, all speaking in unison, asking the same impossible thing. Four of them have engineering books mixed in with the receipts and newspaper, are using the register for scratch paper. One of them is Pima. He listens all the way to *bad skin*, and then is thinking about one of his relatives, lost too, still the same age in his mind as the last time he saw him.

I leave him to it, but as I'm walking out he whispers something through the cage: *liver messiah*.

By the time I turn back, he's at his calculations again.

That night it's my shift, and I tune in some old military sitcom Dad hasn't seen since Nixon. He says it's been waiting out there for him in the roar and hiss of the ionosphere for years, and I pretend to watch it with him but am really watching him the same way he watched that ATM: waiting for something inside to break. The doctors say two weeks, two days, two hours, have I checked him in the last couple of minutes? Still full of the sitcom, I stand in the hall and attract the doctors with a cigarette, look at the tile floor and ask them what about an Indian organ donor, and they laugh and trade looks and take the pulse on the inside of my wrist, say if we were on the reservation, maybe, where wrapping your car around a tree is a varsity sport, but not here, no.

The thin, inner wall of my wrist beats against their fingertips, and the next morning it's thrushing in my right ear. Raymond is in the plastic chair beside me, watching Dad. Waiting. Already he's wearing the shoes that go with the slacks and jacket of his borrowed suit. Last night in Dad's military sitcom, when it was down to the last moment where everything could be happy or sad, they used lard to grease the parachute cords, make them unfold properly in whatever foreign climate they were in, and it worked: their silk sails billowed out with air and they floated off into war with biscuits in their mouths, the end of some other joke I never got.

"Nearly dressed?" I ask Raymond, not really wanting an answer, just an excuse to leave, to bum around the nurse's station, whisper what the hotel clerk might have said: *liver messiah*. As one, they hush, pretend not to have heard. "What?" I almost say, but don't. One of them I think nods down to the women's bathroom for me, but then the security guard has a hangover, is tethered to the water fountain between the men's door and the women's. I go in mine, stand on a toilet with my ear to the vent, and hear the nurse whispering to someone else, about me, about my father.

The other nurse says not to report it—me, my question—not to get involved, and then flushes in disgust. She sounds older, like she's seen all this before, and doesn't look away from me when I pass in the hall.

Back in the room Dad's asleep and Charline is rewinding the ATM videotape to watch it again, through the concave bottom of one of the cafeteria glasses. It's supposed to reverse the distortion, cancel the fish-eye lens, make Dad look normal.

Later that day I'm at a shelter with a photograph of him, the way he used to call himself Middle-Sized Plume when he was drinking, so he could fit in the bottle better, but again, nothing. I eat two biscuits and take a cup of coffee with me, and on the way out one of the men whispers it through his matted beard—*liver messiah*—and then it passes from mouth to mouth with all due reverence until one man in BDUs takes me by the elbow, leads me outside, points eight buildings down the street, two doors over, second hall on the third floor.

My father's room.

The clerk gives me the key, a butter knife looped to a frisbee with rawhide. It works. I enter expecting him to be there sitting on the bed in his underwear and shirt, fumbling in the sheets for a cigarette, a phone ringing somewhere down the hall and him tilting his head to it for a moment, then striking a match. When I was twelve and switching seats with him for the police—my beltloop catching on his buckle until we figured it out—that's all he would ever give the officer: his face flared up yellow for a fraction of a second in the matchlight. The speech he would recite from the darkness, telling how I was driving him home because he couldn't, what was wrong with that?

His face against the sterile hospital sheets is the same yellow now.

In his hotel room there aren't any pictures of us to keepsake or long-lost tribal rattles to sell or pinstriped suits for me to wear, just tissues that crumble when I touch them, beer-can ashtrays balanced on every sill and ledge, and sitting in the middle of all of it I picture Thomas out there somewhere, insulating himself with the same stuff, paper and ash and spit, like a wasp, then burrowing back into it, emerging days later—now—to roll into town in the back of a pickup, walk up to the nurse's station and do what none of us can: hold a gun to his head and give Dad a healthy liver, his own.

I laugh quietly, through my nose, and it doesn't happen—
Thomas—and I feel enough like shit for even thinking it that I don't
tell Raymond and Charline about the room, because then they might
think it too, or see me there thinking it. When they ask me where I
got the jacket, though, I lie that it was down at the station, the ambu-
lance left it there when Dad collapsed in the cinderblock interroga-
tion room under the weight of all that suspicion. It's warm.

That night one of the nurses invites us to a party she knows about.
Raymond, wearing the slacks now too, shakes his head No responsi-
bly, gravely, and I lean down to Dad to say goodbye, a ritual now. For
an instant we're cheek to cheek, closer than we have been in years,
and then his hand is at the base of my skull and he's telling me he saw
Him in the hall tonight, His great white coat trailing behind Him,
and I ask him Who? and he says I know already, but He's flying out
in the morning, and the whole time his jaundiced fingers are dancing
over the back of my head, as if programming me.

As we're leaving, Charline tilts her head back to hold the fake
smile on her face and pretends to be a good sport, saying she'll drink
one for him, and we ride with the nurse to one house then another,
stand on the lawn for maybe thirty seconds before going in, so
Laurence, her oldest, can pee in a bush. The steam rises off it. We
don't say anything to each other, and finally she laughs nervously,
wades to the door. I follow.

Inside it's chips and beer and two televisions in two different
rooms. Two more Indians are on the couch, both guys, longhairs, one
beer one water, meaning passenger and driver, and we stare at each
other because we don't know what tribe, and then nod at the last possible instant. Standard procedure. You pick it up the first time a white
friend leads you across a room just to stand you up by another
Indian, arrange you like furniture, like you should have something to
say to each other.

Charline's kids disappear into the tires and illegal garden of the
backyard, and, now that they're safe, she walks through a dream to
the bathroom, to cry the last three days out into someone else's toilet
paper. She was the one who took the picture of Dad in bed, then had
it developed, so we could show it around. I stand guard at the door,
drink the beer that appears in my hand, and talk to a fake-blonde girl
who's going to grow up someday to be a model for a blow-up doll.

Soon enough someone carries her away under his arm and I'm first in line for the bathroom.

"You okay?" I ask, for the people behind me, and the second time the knuckle of my middle finger knocks on the door it swings away and Charline is composed again, slimming her shirt down her side. She has makeup on now, angry lips and bruised eyes.

I walk in behind her and just stand there in the white light, flush for appearances, follow her to the kitchen. The party's already thinning out. Halfway across town my father is dying. Through the kitchen window Laurence and Theode and Kaney are hiding from each other in barrels of rotted seed. Maybe it was one of them the guys at the shelter were whispering about. Maybe there's some way to die in the backyard no one will ever have known about till now.

"What?" Charline says, not looking at them but me, and I turn from her, make the circuit with another beer in hand, come back with the news: our nurse is gone. We don't know how to get back to the hospital, don't have a car to do it in. The two Indian guys are still on the couch, too. We did the nod routine again as I walked through, and this time I held my cup up in passing, teasing the driver. Charline asks the hosts if we can use the phone, and when we can, I stretch it out into the backyard to watch my nephews and nieces, tell the hospital operator my father's room number. It takes Raymond a long time to pick up, and when he does the military sitcom is behind him, roaring and hissing.

"He told me," he says, before I can even get started about directions and cabs and how I'll pay him back.

"What?"

"Where it is."

"I was going to tell you."

In the digestive lull that follows I can see him; he's got the jacket part of the suit on now, and he's leaned over on his knees, holding his head in one hand, the phone in the other, talking behind his hair where Dad can't hear him.

"He thought I was Thomas," Raymond goes on. "He said it'll pay for it all."

It's my turn to digest now: we're not talking about the rented room.

"Start over, Ray," and he does, and it's the fish-eye movie, Dad getting money somehow from the ATM machine, or from the people,

Raymond's not clear. But he has it. It's tied to the bank of the river in a length of inner-tube, knotted at both ends like intestines you cook, a brick pulling it down.

Enough to pay for It. To pay Him.

"Ray," I say, "I don't know," and he doesn't either, or can't say it over a landline, and we leave it at that for now, and after he hangs up I hear someone breathing on the phone, on my end or his I don't know. The old nurse, probably. Not getting involved.

Back inside, it's two in the morning and awkward: the people whose house it is are in the back room playing naked reindeer games, and up front it's just me and Charline and her crashed kids, the two Indian guys of no particular tribe, and about six other people, including the blonde. She's on the end of the couch, to the left of the driver, rubbing his thigh and saying she's a massage therapist, that she shares an office with a licensed hypnotherapist.

We all lean forward for more.

She rubs a little higher on the driver's thigh and spirits his dangly keys out, and with the AA chip I recognize, which explains the water in his hand, she hypnotizes the willing, insists that the lights be low or it won't work. We crowd around her in the darkness, let her voice lull us into submission, suggestion. It works on two of the people, either that or they pass out, and the other three drift off to find a newspaper for some reason, leaving just four Indians and one blonde around the coffee table.

The blonde snaps suddenly for what feels like minutes and in the background, in the hum of the city, I hear it: *liver messiah, liver messiah*, the water lapping at the inner tube. "You know each other," she says to me and Charline and the two Indian guys, and like that we do, we always have, and I understand that AA was court-mandated, part of some bargain, the back end of some offense, and they see my father through my eyes, pickled in a hospital bed, inventing Someone to save him. The blonde leans back into the couch, the keys dangling from her upheld finger, and we watch them long enough that it pushes us deeper, deeper, until the driver leans forward, slips the ring off her finger. We stare at each other with everything already said, the blonde nodding off in the silence, reinflating, and in my peripheral vision Charline and the passenger are doing everything but trading spit.

"I'll watch the kids," I tell her, and she stands shyly, because I'm her brother, but still, in that way she has with her knees together. It makes her narrow hips look more feminine. She doesn't look at me as she leaves, stepping into the wet grass and fermenting seed of the backyard. The passenger follows on tiptoes, because waking the kids will ruin this, and then, as he turns to pull the sliding glass closed behind him, runs his middle finger under his nose sweetly.

I stand but the driver has me by the wrist. Which is fine. All in one motion, I turn, shove him back into the couch. He won't fight me, though, just nods into the backyard. "His damn liver wouldn't last your dad five years," he says, and when I still don't sit, he adds that his wouldn't either. All I'm hearing is *five years*, though. Maybe I'd have a suit by then.

To keep my hands busy, I roll the wheel of my lighter for my last cigarette, casting a yellow glare over the driver's face for an instant too long. On the floor Kaney coughs and stands silently from the jacket she's under. It falls away from her and she's no one, everyone, asleep. I guide her back down by her thin shoulders and the driver and me watch her side rise, rise. I offer the cigarette to him and instead of taking it he asks me something: "You're not Him, are you?"

I hold my smoke in, step quietly to the sliding door, turn the floodlight off. "I don't know," I tell him, careful not to catch his eye in the glass, and he tells me I'm not from around here. I tell him no shit, I can't even find the damn hospital to watch my father die.

"Three weeks ago," he says, "this varsity football star takes it wrong in the gut, and it mashes him up inside bad, like he's going to die, and when no one will give him any of the organs he needs, even after they've flown in all the good doctors, bumped him up on all the lists, shown his face on the news and everything, the security guard at the hospital steps out for whatever security guards do outside at three in the morning, and there's a body laid out naked-ass cold on the asphalt, with a magic marker showing where to cut on his stomach. A dotted line, like. Taped to his forehead is his driver's license. He signed in the right place."

That's where the three people were going earlier: to get a newspaper, see if He got another one.

"You know where the IHS is?" I ask the driver, and he nods, translating it into hospital, and I pat the kids before I leave, then shake the blonde, tell her to listen for them. Her eyes roll open when I sit her up, and her mouth is an O, which is enough like *okay* that I can lie to Charline that she was awake when we left. That I was going to come back for them in Raymond's car. That I was going to find Thomas, tell him to get here if he has to hijack a mail truck. That I was going to buy a suit on credit somewhere, parachute down to the hospital with a biscuit in my mouth. Maybe the nurse is already there, too, at the hospital—*our* nurse. Maybe her beeper went off with an emergency, my father at the PA, offering money for one good liver.

I have to stop him, at least see him. Things are different now.

But we're not going there, either, anymore.

I turn to the driver, slaloming downhill on low-profile tires, the sloped nose of his car inhaling the miles, and he downshifts, nods over the hood at the river, its surface blurry in the light rain, as if just forming. For us. It was him on the phone.

The inner tube is right where Dad said, like a piece of intestine from something too big to wrap my mind around. We remove it cleanly, put it in the backseat, and the whole time I don't say anything, can't. Finally I just make the cigarette motion to my mouth, mutter something about withdrawal. We glide into a convenience store, and before he can stop me, I have the shiny keys, the six-month chip, am strolling the aisles with a handful of crisp twenty-dollar bills. *Five years*, I keep saying, then return to the car with cold cans of beer for my father, for the driver, who holds the first in his hand like a relic, then takes the rest without question, one after another, well into the slick roads and shattering glass of the night, and the only thing that still rises hot in my throat from that time is that for a moment I saw Myself passing in the plate-glass window of the convenience store, My coat trailing behind me, a styrofoam cooler swinging at My thigh, heavy with ice and miracles, the hospital somewhere in the city, around every next corner.

Psycho-narratives

Amy Hill

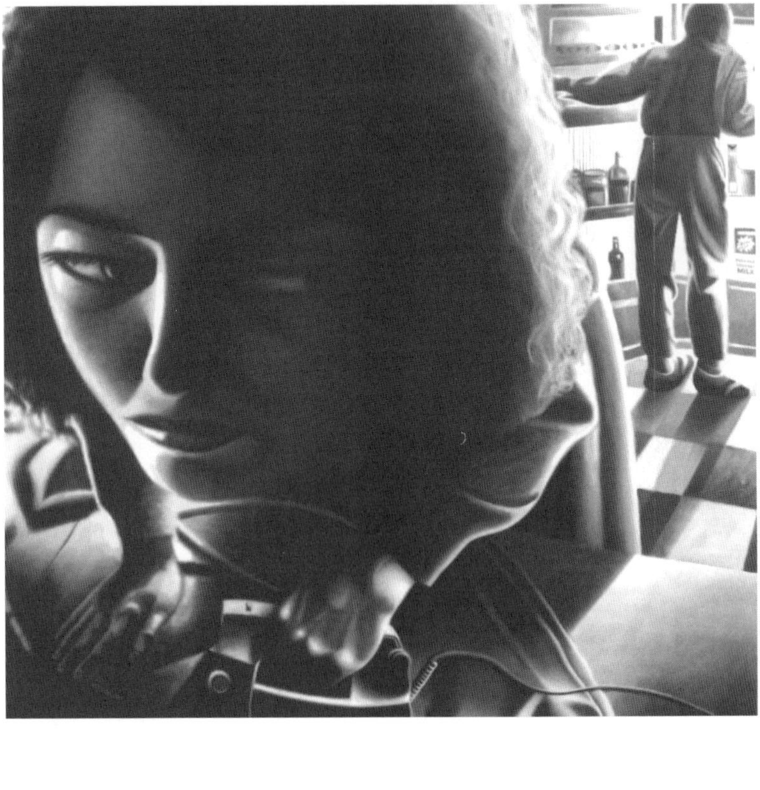
MILK

Time is not constant, it shakes and folds and twists.
Time is not a snake.
The present swallowed by the past.
The future outracing the present.
(Brownstein, page 201)

Enough About Me

Elizabeth Grove

EVERY DAY ANYA SEES THE BOY: FRIENDLESS, BESPECTACLED, husky, a touch, well, spastic. She wonders if spastic is an insult in this case; the school he attends, which Anya passes on her way to work, the Louisa May Alcott School, is supposed to be for children with special needs. But the small number of little men and women who attend it seem not so much to have special needs as they do special appetites, this being their last stop before Hazelden or Betty Ford or someplace where there are euphemisms for "lockdowns."

There they are, congregating before homeroom or whatever it is that begins their day. They have their conversations: fuck fuck fuck fuck fuck. They chain-smoke. They chain-smoke and play hackey-sack. You don't need your hands for hackey-sack—why not keep them busy with something? They make Anya feel old and tired; the small joy she derives from them is that she is not herself a parent staring down the barrel of an adolescence she has helped to create.

Their hair is neon, their clothing doesn't fit—too big, too small— they're pierced in places that seem to Anya to possess a distinct lack of flesh for the task. They take up too much room on the sidewalk where they stage their dramas every morning: clumsy fistfights, some making out, small gestures of collegiality—a shared cigarette, a pat on the back, a general mutant bonding.

Except for the boy. In this palace of losers, the boy is king, which is to say he's in exile even there. He sits on a nearby stoop by himself, making occasional forays to check the bank clock on the corner. His stance is wide and he pitches forward when in motion. His arms swing randomly to keep his balance. But his worst feature, the one that makes Anya turn away and hold her breath as if she were passing a cemetery, is a certain petulance, a certain opaque thickness to his features. Anya knows all too well that this makes one not inclined to like or help him, just two of his special needs among the warehouse of possibilities: like me; help me. It is safe to say the boy's special needs are not being met at the Louisa May Alcott School.

Anya gives him six months before he begins wearing his winter coat throughout summer and completing his conversations with himself out loud.

Everything that Anya has spent her life trying to extinguish, excise, exorcize from herself, burn, cut, bore to death, is in that boy.

When she was in high school on an A Better Chance scholarship, her classmate, Andrew Lumer, fledgling graffiti artist, ran into some boys tougher than he thought he was. They stole his bike, his allowance, knocked him around some. Then they found his fat graffiti marker and drew on Andrew Lumer a black eye, a moustache, and sideburns. They also tried to black out a tooth but Andrew Lumer kept his mouth firmly shut even though or maybe because it kept him from calling out for help.

Indelible, it turned out, was a bit of an overstatement when it came to human skin, but Andrew Lumer's inky bruise and facial hair faded slowly from black to dingy gray before vanishing.

Vengeance, of course, was on Andrew Lumer's mind and on the minds of his friends. That could've been unfortunate, but they went to a Quaker school and were instead encouraged to express themselves in assemblies where they could be guided to a pacifistic point of view, where they could play songs by The Who and talk about anger.

Anya enjoyed The Who and did consider herself a pacifist, mostly because she suspected that in a violent confrontation she would lose and it would be painful. This didn't, however, stop her from imagining a more powerful version of herself beating the living shit out of some real or imagined tormentor.

Still, the boy at Louisa May Alcott keeps her faithful to a nonviolent world view. She's a conscientious objector, always.

Anya lives in New York, she's back, running out of money, gaining weight, trying not to weep on the subway in the mornings because if she starts she will have to check in somewhere and that would make her feel even worse. She works at Think, Inc., where she tries to think as little as possible and that is not difficult. Think, Inc., despite its jaunty name, is a loosely organized group of PhD's with more than the usual flair for pretension. They put out *Think Quarterly*, but are so busy thinking that only two issues have appeared annually for the last several years. The editorial board, headed by renowned analyst Dr. K, likes Anya because she has a master's degree: she's like Cinderella but not too stupid.

Think, Inc. is housed on one floor of a psychoanalytic training institute: the basement. Anya's office is literally a closet; for the first month she would occasionally walk into the other door on her hallway, momentarily disoriented by the floor-to-ceiling book cases full of patient files where her monastic desk should have been. Aside from Anya, Think, Inc.'s only staff member is Jake, who typesets *Think Quarterly* on inadequate software.

In the absence of completed manuscripts to do anything with, Jake puts his feet up, reads Spinoza and Stephen King, and drinks Mountain Dew by the liter. The extra caffeine almost counteracts the THC he's got stockpiled in his body.

Anya has been at Think, Inc. for two months and has fantasized for about seven weeks that she is not a copy editor at all, but a subject in the institute's latest research project. She taps the walls for evidence of microphones, one-way mirrors, cadavers.

"I think I'm losing my mind," she says to Jake one day.

Jake puts his finger carefully on the place where he's stopped reading *Cujo*. "Want a Xanax?" he says.

Anya sits down heavily. "No," she says.

"Let me know," he says.

"No," she says.

Some evenings she goes out to Sheepshead Bay and sees girls from the old neighborhood. Girls she was in school with. Girls who made no effort at academics but who could wax an eyebrow perfectly in one shot. Anya made an effort, got a scholarship, many of them, in fact. Married a boy with no connection to either motherland—

Brooklyn or Russia. Not that that worked. Now she goes to see the girls she can remember; they're all still married, many of them with small children. It doesn't mean they're necessarily happier than Anya is, but she has little patience for their plights and suspects they fabricate their miseries to cheer her up.

"You're so lucky you don't have children," says one. "It really does unspeakable things to the body."

Anya's list of reasons not to have children is long, but bodily damage ranks low on it. It's age, she thinks, not procreation that plays its cruelest joke on form. Age, gravity, and the shrapnel of myriad decisions, all of which include the phrase, "Oh, fuck it . . ."

"So," says Jake sometime during her ninth week at Think, Inc., "you want to smoke a joint?"

"Do you know how old I am?" Anya says. "I'm old enough to be your . . ."

"Sister," Jake says. "You're old enough to be my sister. Maybe my aunt in a nontraditional family."

"Sister," Anya echoes. He's probably right. Think, Inc. has destroyed her mathematical skills, which helps when she looks at her paycheck.

"At least keep me company," Jake says.

In the patient file room she glances around nervously as Jake sloppily inhales next to yellowed onion-skin sheets, the crumbling histories of generations analyzed at the institute. She keeps her hand on the doorknob, imagining the fireball will be sudden and fierce.

Jake stubs the joint out carefully on the metal bookshelves. "Could you watch that?" Anya says. The back of the door is mirrored and she wonders why as she looks at herself become irritable, looks at the silky boyish back of Jake's head. He has a nice neck, too delicate a stem for the rest of him.

"Watch what?" Jake says, looking around. "You have a really cute accent, you know."

"I don't have an accent," Anya says. "I've been here since I was eleven. No accent."

"Uh, okay," Jake says. "Maybe not in the Ukraine." This cracks him up.

"I'm Russian," Anya says.

"What's the difference?" Jake says. He means it.

"I don't have an accent," Anya says again. But she knows it's hopeless. Her ex-husband once told her in exasperation that he couldn't argue with her because when she was angry she stacked up her words with phonetic perfection but no inflection, so that it was impossible to understand what she was saying. She had never believed it was only that.

"You want to go out sometime?" Jake says.

The next day they have a visitor at Think, Inc., an older woman with a bouffant and spike heels who sits herself down at the third empty desk and proceeds to line up prescription bottles wrapped in tinfoil. Anya sees the first one go down and recognizes it: Valium, five milligrams. She looks at Jake, who gestures for her to follow him out into the hallway, and then out a heavily padlocked door into Think, Inc.'s backyard. It is something like freedom.

"That's Dr. K's mistress," Jake says.

"Oh, please," Anya says.

"Really," Jake says. "Okay, she's the executive editor of *Think Quarterly*, but that's because she's Dr. K's mistress. She comes in about once a month to make long-distance calls."

Anya doesn't like these kinds of theories, rejecting them as flabby and misogynistic, but after an hour of listening to the woman chat on the phone, she realizes it's true: fucking. Fucking is the only possible explanation for this woman's presence at Think, Inc.

When Jake gets up again later, Anya follows him out. She likes the backyard he has just shown her. Although the sun is not hitting their scrap of concrete, Anya can see that the sky is a brilliant bright blue. Somewhere not so far from them, the sun is making contact, warming everything in its path. It makes her feel brave and almost happy and when Jake passes her the joint, she shares it with him. From the number of pills the woman inside has swallowed, she figures it's going to be a long day.

Jake looks up and around, the mere movement of his head making Anya feel much more stoned than she is. He scans the buildings above them. "I think," he says, "it's raining snot. Or spit. Or something."

Simultaneously, a beat behind, it's hard to tell, Anya becomes aware of a sound different from the muffled noise of the city. She follows it and high above them she spots the boy sitting on the fire escape of the Louisa May Alcott School.

He's on the stairs, hugging his knees and weeping with no attempt at control. His mouth hangs open and gasps and snorts escape from it. His face is wet from crying; tears drip from his eyes, off the end of his nose, from his chin. The sound is steady: unh-unh-unh.

"Holy shit," says Jake.

"I'll go out with you sometime," Anya says, to fill in the space, to make whatever is happening stop, to keep Jake from being a Good Samaritan, if that's what he has in mind, or maybe it's to keep from having to watch him laugh if that's the other thing he may have done.

When they leave that evening, Dr. K's mistress ahead of them having stumbled toward a cab, Anya sees the boy sitting on the stoop of the school. He seems somewhat recovered, at least he's not sobbing as he rocks and looks through a notebook. A teacher is leaving the school when they walk by, and Anya tries to catch their conversation as the boy starts to speak. "Gotta run, Toby," the teacher says. Anya's sorry she now knows his name.

"Let's go to your place and order a pizza," Jake says. "I live with my parents."

"You do?" Anya says. "Doesn't that interfere? With your lifestyle? With girlfriends? With all the pot you smoke?"

"Not really," Jake says.

It is homey, domestic, this pizza in her small apartment in an outer borough with this man whom she has seen more of than anyone else in months. She started at Think, Inc. in the summer, now they are moving fast through fall. The heat has just started to come up in the apartment, its stale smell reminding her how long it had been dormant.

Anya thinks of the boy and it disturbs her. What is it, she wonders, that separates him from every other zero wandering the city and somehow passing? What lack of style—real or faked, it doesn't matter. What lack of innate grace? What missing ability to convey "fuck you" without even trying? These are microscopic distinctions, it occurrs to her, but the difference is enormous. The leap from that boy to popular bully, that space in between, is so small, she knows. She knows because that space is the scrap of cosmos she happens to occupy, filling it to capacity, feeling it closing in. And now there is Jake, warm and happy and full of pizza, somehow wanting to share it.

Dr. K is on the phone. Anya hasn't spoken to him in a month. "*Exciting* news, Anya," he says. "My book has been accepted for publication. By a mainstream *publishing house.*"

"That's *great*, Dr. K," Anya says, in her best Up with People voice, its tone decidedly faded by noon each day, but it's only nine-thirty and she and Jake have just stumbled into work. Outside, it's sleeting.

"I've left it, a copy, on your desk," Dr. K says. "It will have to be proofed, of course."

"Of *course*," Anya says. She watches Jake start in on his first liter of Mountain Dew.

"I'm not much of a typist, I'm afraid," Dr. K chuckles.

"Of course *not*," Anya says, trying to remain cheerful. She locates the manuscript on her desk, on top of the jumble of patient records she and Jake have been reading aloud to each other, killing time. It's typed on onion skin paper, the place seems to have nothing but, the manual typewriter heavier on the r's than on any other key. It gives the impression, of *course*, of being decades old. But with Dr. K. that could be illusory. She wonders if he's an idiot or just affected, but decides with Dr. K. the distinction is probably illusory too.

"Do you see it there?" Dr. K asks.

"*But Enough About Me, What Do You Think of My Narcissism: An Analyst's Memoir*," Anya recites.

"*Exactly*," Dr. K says. Anya wonders suddenly if he's wearing any clothes on the other end of the phone. But enough about her, she thinks, what would Dr. K make of her thoughts?

Some nights Anya and Jake go to Mr. Mezze in Anya's neighborhood. The beer is cheap and olives and miniature grape leaves are free at the bar. Sometimes the owner—Mr. Mezze himself—maybe remembering his humbler origins, maybe just aware of the overage in his kitchen, sends out borek and spanakopita to them. The phyllo, warm and drenched in butter, makes Anya happier than almost anything she can think of.

"What do you want," Jake says one night.

"I want some moussaka," Anya says. "I'm feeling bold."

OPEN CITY

Jake studies his beer bottle—Latrobe! Anya thinks, it just says Latrobe—and keeps studying it. "I mean, from me," he says finally. "Like, what do you want from me?"

Anya takes a long sip of her own beer while Jake waits for an answer. He has that kind of patience, she's noticed. He seems almost to have forgotten he's asked any question at all. It occurs to her that he is young enough not to know the difficulties what he's asking; in fact, he is so unformed somehow that he wouldn't even know the trouble he would have if she asked him the same.

"I want," she begins, trying to brighten, trying as you would with five-year-olds, convincing them that washing dishes is a really fun game, "I want you to send me flowers for no good reason."

"Okay," Jake says.

The next morning they arrive at Think, Inc. before he does: a dozen shrieking pink tulips. "For no good reason," the card says. "Jake."

Jake lies in bed, the sheets artfully askew, the sun streaming in the windows: it looks almost like something, this warm sunny winter thaw. He smiles lazily at her, stretches. Mid-stretch he shouts, "Ahh-Ahh-*Ahh*! Ahh-Ahh-*Ahh*!" He collapses and plays a little air guitar. Shaking his head, he wails, "I come from the land of a-ice 'n snow, from the . . ."

"That's 'The Immigrant Song,'" he says.

"That's *your* immigrant song," Anya says from the doorway.

"*I'm* not the immigrant," Jake says. "*I* was born here. My mother . . ."

"I know," Anya says. "Your fresh-off-the-boat mother went into labor watching *Chinatown*. That's why your name is Jake. It's a beautiful story."

Jake pats the bed. "Come here," he says. "The sun is doing really weird things to the dirt on the windows."

As for Anya, she came over—already born—with her parents; some foundations liked her and sent her to college; she left her husband by packing a bag and exiting the apartment; she worked in the basement of a nearly defunct psychoanalytic institute. Was it so wrong to feel the facts of one's existence so tersely, as she often thought while rummaging through other people's files; the patients' minutiae poked, prodded, plundered for every nuance: the impure thoughts about the upstairs neighbor, the upset stomach after the pork chop, the dream about the librarian from fourth grade. Yes, Anna surmised, it was wrong. But what was the other choice? To let it rip, all the Slavic heaviness she carries around, built for tragedy somehow, for opera and expensive brandy and an extravagant bubble bath by candlelight where she opens her veins into the warm water. The capacity is in her, long subdued but not quite dead. It's in the architecture of her genes.

"You've got to love your parents," Jake informs her one night. "At least," he says, "you've got to love that they love the American dream."

"My parents don't love the American dream," Anya says, tossing the day's mail into the recycling bag that hangs by her sink. "They love the Soviet dream, which is to be in America drinking better-quality vodka than they get in Odessa."

Jake stares at her like there are things he might dare say. Then the moment passes. He stares instead into the refrigerator he has opened. "I love the American dream," he says, his back to her.

"Not really," Anya says. "You happen to love the New York dream, and that is to somehow live rent-free in two places. But it's all downhill from there."

"You know," Jake says, "what is so wrong with me? I know you've got a long list, but what happens to be at the top of it right now?"

Anya considers this carefully. "You make love like you're happy," she says.

"I am happy," Jake says.

"You make love and it's like Frisbee, it's like soda pop," Anya says. "It's like puppies and bobbing for apples."

"You're insane," Jake says. This seems to Anya like a good place for him to storm out, but he doesn't. He just walks into her bathroom and takes a bath, and not a melodramatic one either. She can hear the splashing.

Anya goes in and sits on the edge of the tub. He's still not unhappy, she notices, though he does pick distractedly at the grout of the tiles. "How should I make love?" he says. "According to you?"

"I don't know," Anya says. "Maybe with urgency. Like your life depended on it."

Jake slides under the water and taps his fingers along the sides of the tub; she knows he's enjoying the deep rumbling sound that makes. He finally comes up for air. "If my life depended on it," he says, "I would've died somewhere between twenty-two and twenty-four."

Dr. K takes Anya out to lunch when she's finished proofing chapter one. He says he wants to do this on a chapterly basis. "That's so kind, Dr. K," Anya says.

"The least I can do, Anya, the very least," he says.

Chapter one is a reverie of the women who have transferentially desired Dr. K, which seems to have been his entire female patient load. Always the professional, Dr. K, declined the invitations, but his imaginings of himself as a more devious psychiatrist are vivid. She's proofed it while reading it out loud to Jake, who's declared it better than *The Stand*. She skims ahead, looking for evidence of the big-haired high-heeled pill-popping mistress, but Dr. K appears to be the model of decorum when it comes to her.

In the slow lunch rush of an Upper West Side diner, Dr. K asks her what her husband does.

"What?" she says.

"Your husband, what does he do?" Dr. K says, sipping his coffee and waiting for her answer.

"I'm not married," she says. "Anymore. I'm not married."

"That's very interesting," Dr. K says. "You look fantastic."

"I'm seeing someone," Anya says.

"You don't say that like you mean it," Dr. K says.

Of all the indignities Anya imagines herself to have suffered, of all the ways that she once thought her life would turn out, ways she can't even remember anymore, she knows this, this present, isn't it, that to be analyzed, unbidden, in a warm and greasy diner on a winter's day by an old and horny shrink. Well, this is a low point, she thinks.

And she figures Dr. K has asked for it, so while he devours a Salisbury steak, mashed potatoes, gray green beans, and several cups of black coffee, Anya unburdens herself. She tells him everything: about coming here with no English, about not wanting to be like the other girls, about not wanting to be herself; she goes on at great length about personal diaspora, a term she figures he will appreciate. About Jake and his unrelenting cheerfulness, a cheerfulness bolstered by lots of reefer and lots of beer and lots of sleep and lots of carbohydrates and maybe lots of her. That he has appeared in her life, all over her life, and this seems not to disturb him at all. That there is a boy she sees every day who rips her heart out of her chest. That he rips everybody's heart out and they all respond as they will. What does it mean, anyway, that there are such people in the world, what does that say about God?

Dr. K signals for more coffee. "Do you want my professional or my personal opinion?" he says.

"Is there a difference?" Anya asks. "I've read chapter one."

Dr. K smirks. "Perhaps not. But suffice to say, there are really only two kinds of people in the world," he says. "Those who find the suffering of the sufferers stupid because they're too stupid to know they shouldn't suffer, and those who find the non-suffering of the non-sufferers stupid because they're too stupid to know they should be suffering."

"Okay," Anya says. "Sure."

"It's a dilemma," Dr. K says. "But what did you think of my book?"

Back at the office, Jake looks up from Dr. K's manuscript. "Did you read chapter seven?" he asks.

"Nah," Anya says. She tries to consider Jake in a new way, as a complicated person in his own right, if not in hers, as a person who has concerns, surely, even if they're invisible to her. She'd spent the walk back to the office along Central Park in its winter starkness telling herself that Dr. K couldn't be right. What kind of analyst tells you there are only two kinds of people in the world? Perhaps, having said all she had said, she had cleared the way for something new, for her and Jake as something, if not romantic, then at least plausible.

"That's good," Jake says. "Chapter seven. I was worried about you."

They smoke a joint right in the office. The mistress won't be back for a month, they decide, her most recent visit having been a few days ago. That they do no work, that they mock confidentiality statutes up and down the line, that they are slowly withering away in a basement is such an open secret that even its openness needs to be hidden from no one. They decide to leave work, such as it is, early, go back to Anya's apartment and turn up the heat and order Chinese food. They lock up the basement and hit the street with all the school children, walking through the wall of their cigarette smoke.

When Anya peeks down the tunnel to see if the train is coming, she sees instead the boy, one foot in front of the other, on the yellow caution line. She knows he doesn't have the motor control, gross or fine, for that kind of stunt. As soon as it occurs to her—magical thinking, Dr. K would accuse—the boy plops onto the tracks.

He lands on his knees.

His howling begins immediately.

And then he is running sloppily, stumbling away from the direction the train will appear. He shrieks, shrieks that are a long time coming, that go far beyond his immediate circumstances, dire as those might become in a few moments.

Anya watches him, made small by his descent down to the tracks, and feels chilled, sick, and like him, that the world has suddenly gotten much worse in one thoughtless second. She looks at Jake, and he is slightly purple, stoned and stupid, under the fluorescent lights of the station, propped languidly against the blue post. "Oh my God," Anya says. "Do something."

"What?" Jake says. "I'm not going down there."

She takes another look down the long tunnel. There is no train coming. Other passersby are beginning to notice what has happened and they are trying to shush the boy to communicate something, anything, to him. His schoolmates, who have clustered near Anya and Jake, curse and point. "You have to," Anya says. "Get to him. Do something."

"Fuck me," Jake says slowly. "I'm no hero."

Anya moves toward Jake to shake him into some kind of action, but when she grabs his shoulders they feel thin under his thin winter coat. She practically outweighs him, she realizes, she is more substantial, a larger woman than he is a man, stronger. A plan seems to be in action down the tracks but Anya doesn't want to see. She keeps her hold on Jake, buries her head into his thin neck, while they stand, both of them, under Columbus Circle, and wait for braver people to come to the rescue.

Why the Long Face?

Craig Chester

IT HAS BEEN SAID THAT MOST BEAUTIFUL BABIES MATURE INTO unattractive grown-ups. I'm not sure who started it but I have found this old wives tale to be woefully untrue. One look at the adult Brooke Shields and that falsehood is blown to beautiful bits. There are exceptions who contribute to the myth, of course—Johnny Whitaker, Shirley Temple, and, of course, the unlucky looking Baby Jane Hudson, among others.

I was a cute baby. No, make that adorable. Better yet, make that delectable. People literally wanted to eat me. My parents would hide all condiments when hungry guests arrived, terrified that their precious baby boy would be doused with Tabasco sauce and swallowed whole like an oyster.

I learned from an early age that cuteness has its advantages. Before I was five, I already knew what my "good side" was in photographs and I worked that right angle for years. Then, around age eleven, the ghastly headaches began.

The doctors didn't know why these headaches racked my tiny little head but believed them to be the logical result of a nasty concussion I had received recently at the hands of my younger sister Kim.

While happily playing with her dolls one day, Kim had a Vietnam-veteran-type flashback of some repressed brotherly cruelty of mine. Dazed and overwhelmed by near total recall of this incident, she fell into a hypnotic remembrance and decided to take justice into her own six-year-old hands pronto.

After rummaging through my father's trunk of music equipment, she discovered the perfect weapon—a leaden microphone. Carrying the weighty blunt instrument in one hand, her baby doll in the other, Kim searched the house, trance-like—in full vigilante mode.

While quietly watching my favorite show, *The New Zoo Review*, I was doing something my parents, had they been home, would certainly have reprimanded me for—lying, stomach on the living room floor, chin propped on palms, with my eyes six inches from the TV.

Upon seeing me, Kim sensed a perfect opportunity. Moving with all the swiftness and sense of purpose her chubby little legs could muster, she approached me from behind. Overweight for her age, she was not a weak child by any means. Even though she was five years younger than I, Kim always won in our fights, either by sitting on me, body slamming me, or resorting to the Hiroshima finale of brother-sister wars—farting point-blank in my grimacing face.

The last thing I remembered was Freddy the Frog. Freddy was my favorite cast member of *The New Zoo Review* and to this day, I blame him and Speed Racer for making me gay.

As I lay facedown on the shag carpet, a lump forming on the top of my head, Kim went back to her bedroom where she resumed playing with her many baby dolls, satisfied deeply.

When my mother walked into the house, arms full of groceries, she saw her only son unconscious on the living room floor. Dropping the groceries that were the barrier between us, she ran over and chose a most effective tactic of awakening me from my stupor—more hitting. I woke up as Rita Moreno screamed, "Hey you guys!" on *Electric Company*.

When my headaches began shortly thereafter, doctors assumed it was the result of this concussional act of sibling revenge. But something was occurring besides headaches when, for no good reason except crap genes, my eleven-year-old face began to warp like an LP left inside a hot car.

At first, the change was subtle. It is not uncommon for a child's face to strain under the influence of budding pubescent hormones. Most children go through a somewhat ugly phase at puberty, a normal burst of pimples and awkward looks. But when my teeth began to turn—to the point of having two front teeth completely sideways—we all knew something was amiss.

My face then began to grow longer, as if melting, elongating into an exaggerated frown. While my lower jaw stretched downward, my upper jaw stopped growing completely at eleven, leaving upper adult teeth nowhere to go but sideways as they struggled to make themselves known.

As the upper and lower jaws tried in vain to formulate a bite, my nose bent—another symptom of a failing infrastructure. My stretched-out face endured enormous effort to keep my lips together. Imagine a perpetual yawn while trying to keep your mouth shut— this was my daily condition, and through this misshapen expression I lived out my entire adolescence.

Eventually my parents had to accept that Craig, their little boy whose epicene beauty inspired face-pinching and veneration, was turning into a monster before their eyes. By fourteen, I looked like a Picasso sock puppet with pimples.

At sixteen, headaches had become a way of life. It was not possible for me to have a conversation without the pop pop popping of my dysfunctional and strained jaw sockets. Eating was also a loud and laborious demonstration of human sound effects.

Constantly teased and mocked, I had learned to walk the halls of school facedown, staring at my shoes, bearing in mind that at any moment I could look up and surprise an unsuspecting and previously unexposed pupil to the horror of my mug.

Gay, painfully shy, socially retarded—there were already obstacles to overcome before deformity. As my face melted, the only features that remained unscathed were my eyes. Through those blinking receptacles, all of teen man's inhumanity to teen man would be recorded for posterity.

"Frankenstein!"

"Gila monster!"

"Ostrich face!"

My dreams of being an actor began to dissolve with every glance in the mirror. The loss of that dream was devastating, for I had only one desire in life—to be a serious actor. Instead, nightmarish visions began creeping into my deformed head: of skipping through Disneyland obscured as Mickey Mouse, of playing "the creature" in low-budget horror movies.

"Why don't you think about writing or journalism, Craig," my drama teacher, Ms. Peveto, quipped. "No one will pay money to see that face on a big screen. I know it's harsh, but I'm just trying to help you be realistic."

Ms. Peveto was just being realistic. My senior year, I won best actor in the state of Texas's National Forensic League's drama competition for enacting a monologue from Paddy Chayefsky's *Marty*—a play about an ugly man who longs for an equally repulsive woman. Ms. Peveto had brought the material to my attention, attempting to use unfortunate looks to my advantage dramatically.

Even after beating out nearly a thousand other student actors to win state, Ms. Peveto still felt it her duty not to let my hopes get too high. I had been written off as the least likely to succeed in her glass menagerie of concubines. Unfortunately, it never occurred to her that the pained existence of an awkward outcast might lend itself to conjuring up deep emotions necessary for a good acting performance. I still believe, to this day, that lesser attractive people are better actors than beautiful ones. Hollywood fights tooth and nail to deny this truism, fooling themselves into believing that cheerleaders and jocks are just as talented as dorks. But it's a lie. The ugly people are better actors and it will always be that way.

Around fifteen, it was decided that I should get braces. It was now an established fact that I would be an ugly person in life, and I had begun to accept the face I inhabited as my own. While we could do nothing about my long features, the least we could do was fix those crooked teeth.

While waiting in the examination chair for my soon-to-be orthodontist, Dr. Dougherty, I was excited. In my mind, anything he could do to help my hideous appearance would be a godsend. After examining my mouth, he grabbed my face and asked me to open and close.

Pop, pop, pop.

As usual, the popping gave birth to a headache. As I winced, Dr. Dougherty called my mother over.

"We are going to have to send him to a specialist. There's something seriously wrong with his bone structure and his jaw sockets. I know an excellent maxillofacial specialist," he said.

"Well, okay. But I don't see how getting a facial is gonna help what's wrong with him," my mom replied.

Not quite knowing what to make of this, my mother took me to see the man who would change my life forever—a man whose name seemed the height of irony considering the religiosity pervading my waking world—Dr. Sinn.

Within seconds of seeing me, he diagnosed my condition right off the bat.

"Long Face Syndrome" is genetic, he told us. The only way to fix it is massive amounts of reconstructive surgery—a painful and grueling process that would require no less than a year of my life. He said it was not classified as cosmetic surgery per se, because of my straining jaw sockets. If I didn't have the surgery, it was very likely that my jaw joints would eventually wear out in my thirties—causing a form of lockjaw.

He pulled out before-and-after pictures and if my jaw could drop any lower, it would have. There they were—people who looked as ugly as I did—on the left. And on the right—a completely different face bearing little resemblance to the one that preceded it.

I was elated.

"He'll have to wait till he's eighteen to have the surgeries done—when his bones are fully developed," Dr. Sinn said.

The three-year wait seemed insurmountable from my teen perspective. I wanted him to put me under the knife right then and there, ripping my mouth out and replacing it with a Farrah Fawcet smile.

Beyond the three-year wait, the other obstacle to this magical process of transformative surgery was the cost—thirty thousand dollars. It was not covered by insurance.

My family vacillated between lower and middle class so it was decided that the money issue would be dealt with once I approached eighteen. In the meantime, Dr. Sinn told us, I should go ahead with braces as planned.

Almost immediately after this, my father fell upon hard times financially. Having left a steady job at Nestle to open his own food brokerage, his new business was not a success and hard times just got harder. The prospects of a thirty-thousand-dollar operation began to seem less and less likely.

Meanwhile, I had begun to collect *GQ* magazines, looking at all the strong chins, the chiseled cheekbones, barely able to contain my hope that someday soon I would also have a chin that I could sharpen a knife on. But when my father's business began struggling, paying the rent began took precedence over luxury items like chins and cheekbones.

Knowing that my fate rested on our financial stability, I began to obsessively monitor my parents' spending. All amenities were a potential barrier to my future.

We Chesters were an empathetic lot. It was not uncommon for a wayward soul to be spending Christmas Day with us. Whether it was a divorced middle-aged woman without a family, an elderly woman similarly alone, or a young runaway down on her luck, our home became the land of broken toys, much to my chagrin. And with every customer served, every dollar spent, I saw my hopes and dreams fade.

While unwrapping yet another new shirt Christmas morning, I could contain my repulsion at my parents' generosity no longer. I stood, holding up the shirt as if it was radioactive.

"I don't need a new shirt! I need a new *face!*" I cried, running to my room and slamming the door.

I would have certainly gone nude for those three years if it meant putting that clothing budget toward my future good looks.

After high-school graduation, I auditioned for Southern Methodist University's Ivy League Theater department. The head of the theater department called my father to tell us I had been accepted into the esteemed program but that he felt I didn't actually need the training they offered. Instead, he thought that I was ready to go straight to New York and start working. There was only one problem.

"That face. It's going to be hard for him with that face," the man said.

My father Cecil had always secretly wanted to be a rock-and-roll star and, if he couldn't fulfill his aims for fame and fortune, he decided to do whatever it took to grant me my wishes of being an actor.

Knowing he could not afford the hefty price tag of the operation, my father called Dr. Sinn and said he wanted us to go ahead with the surgery anyway. He told Dr. Sinn that truthfully he could not afford it, but that he would find a way somehow and to bill him for the operation.

With that, my father did something that saved my life as surely as if he had thrown himself in front of a speeding train.

I was admitted a month later to St. Paul's Hospital in Dallas for the first of a series of operations.

The first surgery would require breaking my upper palate, which had stopped growing at eleven, and resetting it to adult size proportions. The second and third procedures would be the most dramatic and performed simultaneously to cut, bread, and reset my upper and lower jaws into some semblance of a face.

After the first operation, I woke up in the recovery room. The first thing I noticed was that there was no access to the roof of my mouth. Instead of a palate, there was a brace of metal. The taste of blood and metal made me gag. Then I saw the shiny little key dangling from my father's fingers.

Every day for a month, the shiny key would be inserted into a small hole in the retainer that occupied the upper half of my mouth. With every turn, my malleable palate would expand, ever so slightly, until a full inch existed between my two front teeth. The device was called an "expansion retainer unit" and it gave my mouth a six-year evolutionary jump from the eleven-year-old palate I had been left with. Once the gap existed in the roof of my mouth, the teeth were moved into a perfectly straight row, filling the one-inch gap gladly.

Once the roof of my mouth was as wide as the bottom, it was time for the serious operation to take place.

Being that I would be undergoing a grueling twelve-hour surgery first thing the next morning, Dr. Sinn required me to check into St. Paul's Hospital the night before.

Meanwhile, I imagined what my new face would look like. The greatest and only fear inspired by the surgery was that no one, not even my doctor, knew what the end result would be until after the surgery and the swelling had reduced. But I didn't care. I could come out looking like the title character in *The Creature from the Black Lagoon*, gills and all, and I still felt it would be an improvement over what I had looking back at me in the mirror.

The next morning, my parents by my side, I was wheeled into the operating room where I would spend the next twelve hours. I moved myself onto the table, fully awake until a nurse inserted anesthetic into my arm.

Looking up, I saw my reflection in a lighting fixture. I took a long last appraisal of the face that had betrayed me. *Good riddance.* Like someone in an abusive relationship who has reached their breaking point, I felt no melancholy, no sentimentality at saying goodbye.

As I slipped away, the image of my face grew more and more distant until, eventually, I was gone.

The first thing I saw when I woke up in the ICU was our preacher, leaning over me, peering through coke-bottle-horn rimmed glasses and sporting his usual gray pompadour.

I struggled to speak. Nothing came out.

My mother came into frame.

"Honey, your jaws are wired shut. There's a plastic bite plate in between your teeth so not even air can pass through. You can't talk or eat, but you have a beautiful chin!" She smiled.

After that brief return from the astral plane, I lapsed back into unconsciousness. I woke up the next day with a sharp shooting pain zipping out the tip of my penis as a stereotypical and emotionally stunted nurse pulled on my catheter with glee.

I have since learned that nurses are much like stewardesses. They are employed to make you feel as comfortable as possible but nearly always wind up doing the opposite. I have formulated this opinion not by unkind prejudice but by a litany of experiences where the medical establishment has failed me miserably. I am of the school of thinking that the customer (or patient) is always right, and have been known to scream, throw Jell-O, and behave in a most undignified manner in order to get the care I need for myself.

I was moved from ICU to a hospital room, lapsing in and out of consciousness and deplorably nauseated from the anesthetic.

Once in my room, I sat up in bed with a start, my mouth watering in anticipation of vomiting. The thought seemed so appealing at that moment, so satisfying. Then I realized that, with my mouth wired shut on a plate, there would be nowhere for it to go but right back down.

My mother intuited my state and approached me brandishing wire clippers.

"Do you have to throw up, honey?" she asked as she snipped the wire cutters together in anticipation.

"The doctor showed me how to cut your wires if you need to throw up," she said. "Only thing is, if we snip the wires, you'll have to go back into surgery and have everything reset."

Having no interest whatsoever in repeating the past two days in intensive care, I instead focused on the nausea-calming pattern of the room's wallpaper—a blueprint of delicate little flowers designed to placate recuperating nerves such as mine.

"You sure you don't need to throw up?" my mom relented, much to my chagrin. It is common knowledge that, when in a state of potential 'heave-ho', the last thing you want from those around you is a preoccupation with your queasy predicament.

"'Cause if you need to throw up, I got the wire cutters right here!" she persisted.

Pretty little flowers. A constellation of sweet little blue pansies. Ahhh. I can do this. I don't have to throw up. WHY WON'T SHE BE QUIET?

"You should try not to throw up if you can keep it down. 'Cause if do, you could choke on your own vomit. It'd probably just come right through your nose and then you could suffocate on your puke."

As these words brought me to the brink, I desperately commanded my mother to stop talking about vomit. Having no way to speak, however, I made a motion toward my mouth as if zipping it—indicating that I needed silence desperately.

"What? You're ripping something from your mouth? What does that mean? You need me to cut the wires? Are you gonna throw up? Gonna throw up? Honey, are you gonna throw up?"

I looked at her and made a muffled noise as I covered my mouth with both hands. Taking this gesture completely the wrong way, my mother lunged at me with the wire cutters, prepared to save my life from my stomach.

Just then, a nurse entered the room, stopping dead in her tracks upon seeing my mother mounting the bed, brandishing wire cutters toward my face.

"Oh my God! What are you doing!" she cried, surely thinking that some strange woman was attacking me, which was not entirely untrue. The nurse then saw the mush that comprised my face and I saw her become as nauseated by my appearance as I felt.

It then occurred to me that in the few minutes I had been awake and fighting my queasiness, I had not yet seen my new face. I noticed a hand mirror near a sink and motioned for the nurse to bring it to me.

The nurse looked conspiratorially at my mother.

"Oh, honey, why don't you rest? You just woke up!" my mother said. I could tell she was covering something up, trying to protect me from the image the mirror would reveal.

Suddenly, I panicked. *Could my looks be worse than before?* My heart raced in anticipation of seeing my new visage. I climbed out of bed to go get the mirror myself, but was too weak and returned. I noticed that my head felt remarkably *heavy.*

"Honey, you just had major surgery. Now, the doctor said it's gonna be a while till the swelling goes down and—"

"MMMM! MMMM!" I shouted as I pointed to the mirror. My mother knew she couldn't keep it from me forever.

She looked at the nurse, who then gingerly brought over the pink-handled looking glass. I took it from her and, after a blinding flash of reflected sunlight, turned it around to face me.

My eyes fluttered with disbelief as I stared at the fiend before me.

Gigantic, balloon-like, cartoon-like—my face and head were swollen to massive, inhumane proportions.

I pulled the mirror at arms length, trying to frame the enormity of my head within it. Little beady eyes peered out of swollen cheeks so large that my nose ceased to exist. Dried blood caked nearly every orifice, from nostrils to mouth to ears.

But the most disturbing feature was the color of my flesh—a jaundiced yellow, swirled together with blue, black, and purple. My head was, quite literally, the size of a pumpkin. But underneath inches of puff, I could discern a definite chin that had not been there before.

My nausea returned. I dropped the mirror and it broke. Seven years of bad luck began.

While the nurse gave me intravenous codeine and anti-nausea medication, I drifted off into a posttraumatic stupor. It wasn't over. It had just begun. The doctor told me a year would pass until all the swelling was completely gone and my new face revealed itself. It would eventually take over two years till the last vestige of puffiness abandoned me.

After several days of recuperation, Dr. Sinn decided I could be moved home. I climbed into a wheelchair, and the nurse wheeled me out into the hallway toward the hospital exit.

Upon entering the hallway, it began. People stared. Jaws slackened, gaped. Mothers grabbed their children protectively as the Pumpkin- Headed Beast breezed through the corridors of St. Luke's.

I half expected the hospital visitors to grab torches and chase me out of town.

My first night home, the nausea was overwhelming. Trooper that she is, my mom slept next to my bed, on the floor, clutching the wire cutters in case of an emergency upchuck that might asphyxiate her beloved son.

My mother had always been such an amazing nurse, which is precisely why no professional nurse has ever lived up to my expectations. Anytime I was sick, there she was, no matter what the hour or her own condition.

Growing up, I rather liked being sick. Being sick meant getting attention, and attention made me feel loved. It took me thirty years and several therapists to eventually realize that pity was not the same thing as love, and that there are dynamics suitable to a mother-child relationship which are unsuitable to any other interpersonal relationship. I tried for years to squeeze sympathy from friends and lovers, thinking that pity meant love. Now I realize that the attention garnished from sympathy only makes people think you are weak.

Being that my mouth was wired shut, I obviously could not eat. Between my two front teeth, near the gum, there was a tiny gap barely large enough to accommodate, let's say, a needle. Through this opening, this tiny portal, I would have to feed myself on a liquid diet for eight weeks. Also, any and all medications would be fed through this pinprick of a hole—mostly liquid codeine and anti-inflammatory drugs.

While I survived on a steady diet of apple juice and Gatorade, I was dreadfully weak. I was forced to continuously drink for fear of dehydration. Every waking moment found a straw in my mouth. Being that the miniscule gap between my two front teeth was the only passageway for nourishment, I was not able to sip anything that possessed even a speck of food. No pulp, no granules of any kind would make it past the pinprick that was my lifeline.

Regardless of this fact, it became a personal mission for my devoted mother to not exclude me from family meals or occasions. I was made to sit at the dinner table, almost nightly, while I watched in contempt as my father, mother, and sister gorged themselves on pot roast, chicken and dumplings, and sloppy joes. Knowing this must be a unique kind of hell for me, my mother took it upon herself to set aside my dinner portions and puree them into a frothy broth. She would have pulverized every conceivable food known to man.

"Dinner's ready!" she would cry from the kitchen.

Then, moments later, the roar of the Cuisinart would fill the house. Despite her efforts, it was a rare occasion that the roast beef, still warm from the oven, would be ground up small enough to make it past my tiny feeding hole. Usually I would take a couple of sickening sucks, only to have the river log-jammed by a stray piece of beef or chicken pulp.

They say Einstein's theory of insanity is to repeat the same mistake and expect different results. Those eight weeks, Cuisinart could have used that slogan for their newest ad campaign.

The insanity reached its apex when, for my nineteenth birthday, my mother pureed my birthday cake. The end result of pureed birthday cake is very much like what birthday cake begins as—batter. Sipping one's birthday cake through a straw might be a nice idea, but there's a reason people bake cakes instead of drinking them.

During my birthday, my extended family decided to pay me a visit to survey the damage.

My grandma, or Nee Naw as we called her, lived in a trailer park in Denton, Texas, just one hour north of our brick-and-mortar abode in Coppell, with her daughter, Aunt Carol, and Aunt Carol's daughters Angela and Shandra. Relations between my mother and her sister had been strained for years. Centering on the fact that my aunt and her daughters could not keep a man, and on the fact that my mother had kept hers, their jealousy of my parents' marriage drove them nuts.

The other thing that perturbed my aunt was that she highly and vocally disapproved of the way my mother raised my sister and me. A huge supporter of beating children senseless if they misbehaved, Carol thought her sister a wimp for not taking the belt to Kim and me on a daily basis. My mother was not a violent woman by nature, thank God. But whenever we would visit our cousins, it was not uncommon for Aunt Carol to beat the holy crap out of them in front of us with unbridled joy.

To anyone even remotely familiar with human psychology, it's obvious that this pattern of abuse is destined to repeat itself, "sins of

the mother" and such. That the abused had become the abuser made
itself painfully clear one day.

One day when I was a small boy, I was playing with my cousin and
her dolls when Angela, five, reacted violently to her kitty after it had
scratched her painfully on the arm.

Picking up the cat by the tail, Angie swung the furry tomahawk
over her head several times before hurtling it full force against a bedroom wall. Amazingly free of any serious injuries, the cat fled quickly and Angela instead chose to beat her dolls by default.

"Mommy is very mad at you! VERY MAD! AAHHH!" she
screamed as she whooped a Cabbage Patch Doll's ass.

People talk about the sad life that gays lead. Well, no amount of
lonely promiscuity could compare to the misery and suffering of
many heterosexual couples living in rural parts of this country. I wit-
nessed many of my female relatives give birth to blameless children
who go on to be ignored or abused by macho, wretched husbands
and themselves. If anyone has doubts about the virtues of gay par-
enting, I invite them to spend one afternoon in a trailer park with
heterosexuals whose sole qualification for raising a child is that they
got fucked.

Arriving for my nineteenth birthday, my Aunt Carol, Angela, and
Shandra stood before me, gazing at the beach ball staring back at
them. They struggled to contain their laughter at my condition.

"Oh, he looks like a Mr. Potato head!" Shandra giggled.

"Do you think he's gonna ever look normal again?" Angela wondered aloud.

"He looks like he was beaten with an ugly stick!" my aunt laughed.
"It's the Great Pumpkin, Charlie Brown!"

They all burst into laughter as if I wasn't in the room.

I learned early on in this experience that there is a portion of the
human brain that believes if one cannot *speak*, that one can also not
hear. It was common for most who encountered me to talk about me
as if I wasn't there. I had seen this phenomenon before when my
father would host one of his many garage sales. When encountered
with non-English speaking Mexicans, he would often overcompen-
sate for their lack of English by simply talking louder.

"Do you think he's in pain?" Aunt Carol asked my mother. I
reached for my Etch-a-Sketch to write "no" but, as usual, I wasn't able

to write an answer quickly enough to maintain the conversation so they all turned to my mom for an answer.

"No, it's more uncomfortable than anything. He has some nerve damage from the surgery, though. There are spots on his face that are numb and probably always will be. Plus, he lost his sense of smell but they say that may come back."

My sense of smell never did come back.

And I have informed all my loved ones of this, I still receive aromatherapy candles and incense sticks at every birthday and Christmas.

I used to make it a point of reminding the gift-giver of my odd olfactory handicap. Now, when I receive a scented candle, I simply pretend to smell the vanilla or patchouli lustily and thank the person, saying that vanilla or patchouli is my favorite scent of all time. Gift-giving and birthday parties being more for the giver than for the recipient, I don't really mind and I expect nothing less than the same insincerity when I bestow a similarly thoughtless present upon someone.

There are quite a few advantages to having no sense of smell, especially if one lives in New York City as I have for over fifteen years. The aroma of urine mingling with garbage on a hot sidewalk has no power over me. Changing the cat box is a breeze. Morning breath, flatulence, and stinky feet have never been an impediment to intimacy, although I must diligently remind myself that my shoe does not fit on the other's nostrils. Cigar smoke, public restrooms, and rotten eggs fall on deaf nerve endings now.

Of course, like anything, the reverse is also true, for there are many smells that I've secretly mourned since my surgery. Fresh-brewed coffee, Christmas trees, baking bread, and fresh-cut grass have been wistfully longed for. I have also never smelt the varied and sundry aromas of sex, since I lost my smell before I lost my virginity. The scent of another man does not exist for me; pheromones wield no pull of attraction in the game of seduction here.

Many dangers present themselves when one has no sense of smell. I have gotten food poisoning numerous times due to an unawareness of spoiled groceries and have been forced to realize that the ability to smell can also be quite the lifesaver,

For example, there was a time when, for several weeks, I was exhausted beyond belief. Convinced that I had Chronic Fatigue Syndrome, those worries were dispelled when a friend walked into my New York apartment only to immediately inform me that there was a gas leak in my home. Since then, I have thought of purchasing a canary to warn me of such leaks, but instead have opted to host dinner parties to alert me to such noxious emissions. If my guests drop dead over the soup, the pilot light must be out.

While I had lost my sense of smell and my ability to speak for two months, I could watch others do both. After my cousins had marveled at the Great Pumpkin, my grandma sat down next to me on the couch.

Being that we rarely had these grandma-grandson powwows anymore, she decided to seize this moment of muteness from me and share some rather startling observations.

"I know you're gay," she whispered, looking around the room so as not to be heard.

My eyes blinked back at her, stunned. Not just by what she was saying, but by the fact that she was breaking my relatives' cycle of assuming that I was as deaf as I was mute.

"Don't say anything, let me talk."

As if that were an option.

"Now, I know the Bible says it's a sin and all—but," she looked around again to ensure total privacy, "I think all your mom's Jesus talk is just a lot of horse shit. I mean, I've known lots of gays in my day. You know I've lived a full life and I know your momma don't approve. But life ain't about sittin' in a church. It's about drinking and smoking and carrying on—living! When I was with Merle—"

My grandmother Gaylon had briefly dated the very young and struggling country-western singer named Merle Haggard. Riding around in the back of his pickup truck from honkey tonk to honkey tonk, she felt a kinship with performers and sympathy for the many paradoxes of show people. She understood my dreams of stardom like no one else in my family. If she had married Merle, her name would have become Gay Haggard, a name which, on occasional, I have felt the dyslexic embodiment of myself.

"Well, Merle didn't believe in any of that crap, and the Jesus freaks tried to shut him down, saying he was singing sin songs and all. Now, your momma, she grew up around all my crazy, hell-raisin' men and now she's just trying to make meanin' outta the crazy mess that life is. You know as well as I do that religion skips a generation.

"Now, I'm not saying I don't believe in nuthin'. My momma's spirit used to visit me after she was dead. She was a full-blooded Cherokee, you know. So I believe there's something out there. Plus, there was that one time, when I saw a jar of peanut butter unscrew its lid all by itself. Well, I just about had a conniption fit over that. So, I believe in that stuff 'cause I've seen it with my own eyes—that Skippy jar shown me there's somethin' more.

"But I bring this up 'cause there ain't nuthin' wrong with what you are. Hell, I've known you was a queer the first time I seen you throw a ball!"

She laughed uproariously but was silenced as hilarity evolved into a smoker's cough.

"Now, your momma and daddy tell me that you're planning on moving to New York to be an actor once all this face swellin' goes down. I think you should. Course, your momma doesn't want you to leave Texas. Hell, she never wanted you to grow up in the first place. But me, I've always thought I coulda been a movie star had I been so inclined. So I want you to remember just one thing when you get to New York: if anyone tells you that you can't make it in show biz, you just tell em: 'Hide and watch'! Okay, now I gotta get in that kitchen and fry up the okra. Remember—'hide and watch'!"

Over the next eight weeks, my family took turns confessing to me the resentments each had for the other. I secretly said little prayers to the makers of the drug codeine, wherever they may be. Had it not been for that purplish drug sucked through a straw between confessionals, I doubt that I would have been able to bear it.

My aunt Carol, or "Auntie," as I called her way past the age a man might call his aunt "Auntie," sat down and torched up one of her low-tar Pall Malls next to her daughter Shandra and me. I took a sip of codeine, prepared to be ignored fully.

"Well, thank God they fixed him. 'Cause that long face was an eyesore," my Auntie snickered.

"I think his new face kinda looks like Elvis—when he was real bloated-like," Shandra observed, also ignoring the fact that I could hear. "God, he looks really weird. His face almost looks fake—like foam rubber." Shandra spoke in a thick Texan accent, even though she grew up in California, like me, and had only been in Texas for two years.

"Dinner's ready!" my mom cried out. A moment later, the blender started.

The entire family gathered in my parents' dining room in front of a huge Texan feast of ribs, mashed potatoes, fried okra, and corn on the cob. Being that it was my birthday dinner, my parents insisted that I join them at the table. I rarely got off the couch by this point, not only because I was completely addicted to painkillers, but also because my swollen head weighed 123 pounds and it was hard to support on my eighteen-year-old neck. My mother set a large glass of pureed rib meat in front of me. I took one sip and decided instead to stick to my apple juice.

"Oh, this fried okra is the most delish thing I've ever eaten in my life!" my aunt declared. "Oh, it's too bad Craig can't have any!"

I was into my fifth week of not eating. That's thirty-five days of no food. If we had been on a glacier in the Andes, I would have eaten my entire family and several of my own toes by this point.

"OH! These ribs! AMAZING!" Angela declared loudly.

"Have some corn! Cecil cooked it on the grill in the husks, and it is just remarkable!" my mother boasted.

I sipped. I gnashed my teeth. Sip, sip, sip.

"Oh, Craig, it is just a shame that you cannot eat this food!" Shandra moaned as she stuffed an entire dinner roll into her mouth.

That was it. I couldn't take it anymore. For reasons that I don't quite understand, *bread* was the food that I missed the most during those months of no eating. Warm baked bread. I had assumed I would miss chocolate, French fries, tacos, but bread turned out to be the thing I missed fully.

I got up from the dinner table crankily.

"Now, see! Y'all have gone and made him upset!" my Grandma grunted, a rib dangling from her mouth.

"Well, maybe he's just tired." Shandra said.

"Yeah, he's just worn out—his head is so big, it's hard for him to hold it up," noticed Angela.

"Well, perhaps it's for the best. This food is delicious, but his looks are a little unappetizing!" Auntie whispered.

I turned around to face my family. Picking up a dinner roll, I threw it across the room spontaneously. It unintentionally bounced of my grandma's nose, leaving a small butter stain.

Everyone looked at me. Finally, they saw me. I tried, in vain, to indicate to them that I could still hear. I pointed to my ears, and then pointed to their mouths, demanding that they stop speaking of me as if I wasn't in the room.

I can still hear! I indicated.

"Craig, why did you throw that bun? Oh, I know! You want me to puree some dinner rolls!"

As my mother ran to the Cuisinart with rolls in hand, I grabbed my car keys and snuck out of the house, the sound of the blender concealing my escape. I was tired of being treated like a deaf person and I thought I certainly must have ridiculed deaf people in a past life to deserve this.

Dressed in pajamas, I drove down the road. I had not left the house alone since my surgery and had forgotten that, while my family was used to my pumpkin head and monstrous face, the rest of the world was completely unprepared.

As I drove down the road, passing cars swerved in horror as they recoiled from the gargantuan face passing them in the opposite lane. They would catch only glimpses of my huge head, and I got only glimpses of their gaping terrified looks. But those looks remain a snapshot in my mind's eye.

Too weak and inappropriately dressed to go inside a restaurant, I decided that I would go through the drive-through window at our town's one and only restaurant—Dairy Queen. There I would order a milk shake, something I knew I could drink, although what I really needed was a whiskey.

I approached the Dairy Queen, rolled down my window and pulled up to the speaker. Suddenly, I realized that I could not order since my mouth was wired shut. Not knowing what to do, I decided to throw caution to the wind and approach the pick-up window.

As I pulled up, a sixteen-year-old stoner-type boy with long hair greeted me. Glassy-eyed and most definitely unhappy with his job, the Dairy Queen boy shrank back in dazed horror as my face was revealed in his window. I'm sure to him it must have seemed as if the Elephant Man had migrated to Texas and was dying for a Blizzard

Sundae. It was obvious that he wondered if I was real or some unpleasant acid flashback.

Trying to get what I needed, I took a notepad from my car and wrote on it: "one large chocolate milkshake." I handed it to him and he stood there for a moment as he read my order. Looking from the notes to me, he nodded his head silently. I nodded back and he went off to make my drink.

I felt vindicated. Finally, I had actually communicated to someone. I had been heard. He saw me, heard me, and was not treating me as though I was a deaf mute. A few minutes later, he emerged with my milkshake. He handed me the frothy drink.

He then handed me a piece of paper. I took it from him, confused.

On a Dairy Queen stationary, he had written, "$1.89."

I'm sort of tall and lanky and a bit sickly looking, but I've always thought that the combination of my dark hair, blue eyes, and harsh features might give off the impression of depth. Sure, it might sound dubious, but once or twice I've even found some insecure girl to corroborate this theory.

(Baumbach, page 39)

Drawings

John Körmeling

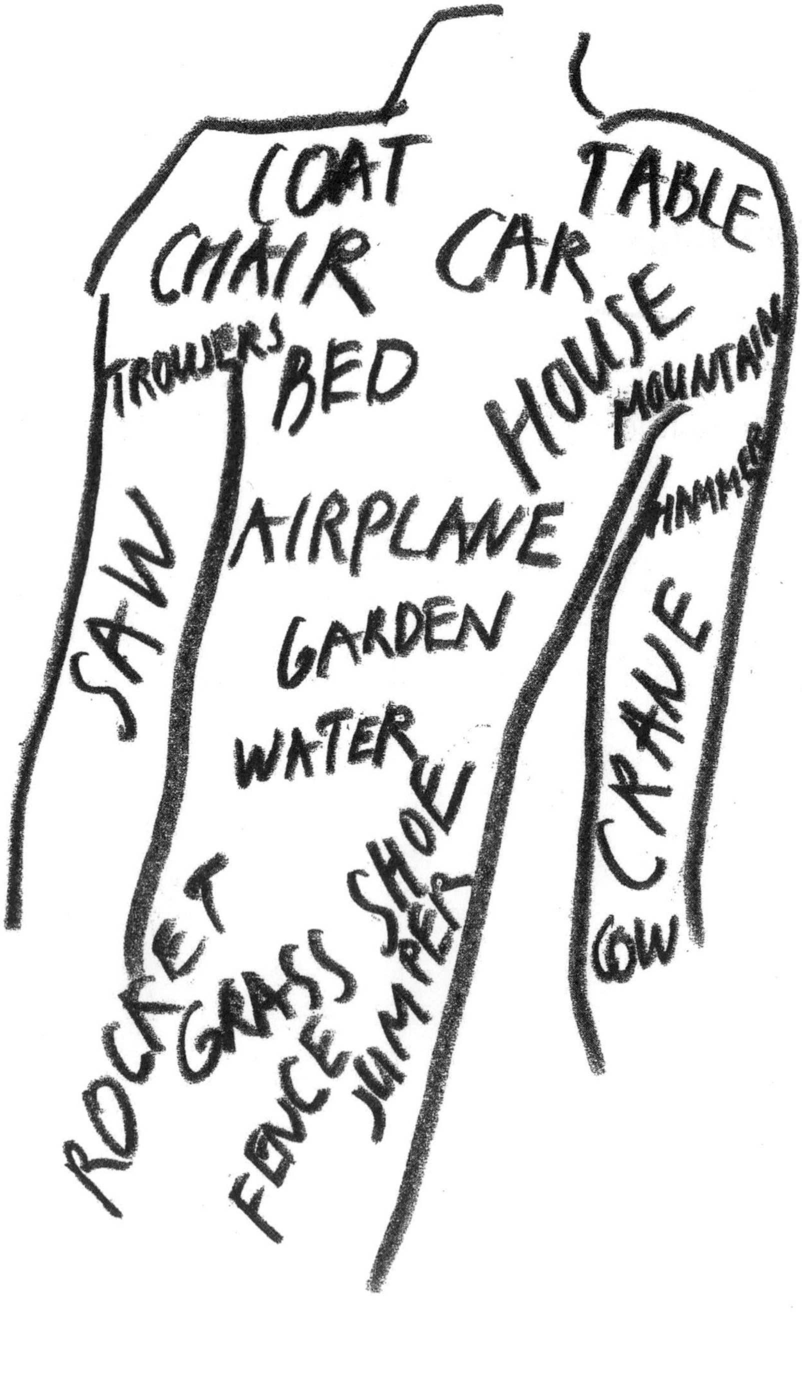

COAT
TABLE
CHAIR
CAR
HOUSE
TROUSERS
BED
MOUNTAIN
HAMMER
AIRPLANE
SAW
GARDEN
WATER
CRANE
SHOE
COW
ROCKET
GRASS
JUMPER
FENCE

TOWNHALL
PRIVATE ROAD
PRIVATE ROAD
PRIVATE ROAD
PRIVATE ROAD
TOWNHALL
PRIVATE ROAD
PRIVATE ROAD
PRIVATE ROAD
PRIVATE ROAD
TOWNHALL
PRIVATE ROAD
PRIVATE ROAD
PRIVATE ROAD
PRIVATE ROAD
PRIVATE ROAD
PRIVATE ROAD
PRIVATE ROAD
PRIVATE ROAD
PRIVATE ROAD
PRIVATE ROAD
PRIVATE ROAD
PRIVATE ROAD
PRIVATE ROAD
PRIVATE ROAD
TOWNHALL
PRIVATE ROAD
PRIVATE ROAD
PRIVATE ROAD
PRIVATE ROAD
PRIVATE ROAD
TOWNHALL

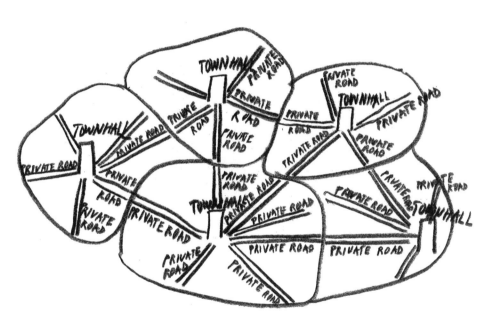

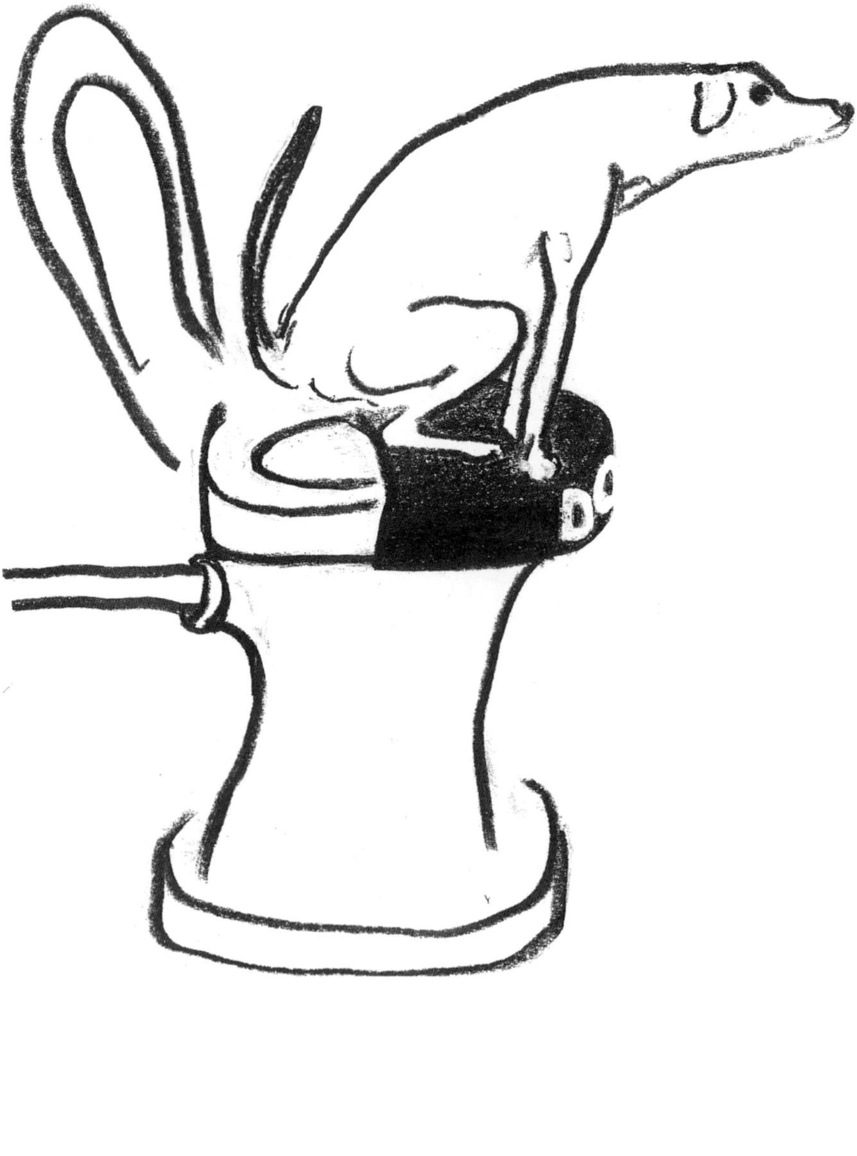
DO

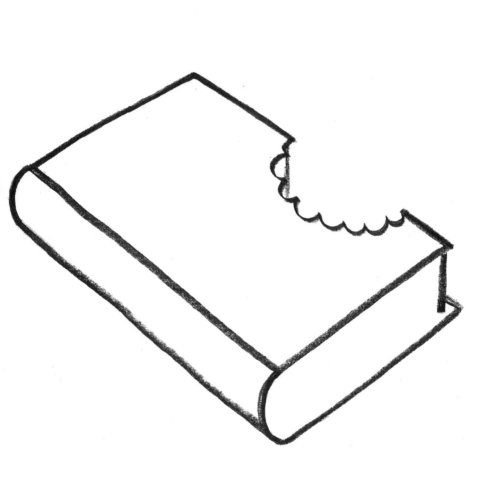

UNIDENTIFIED

•

IDENTIFIED

•

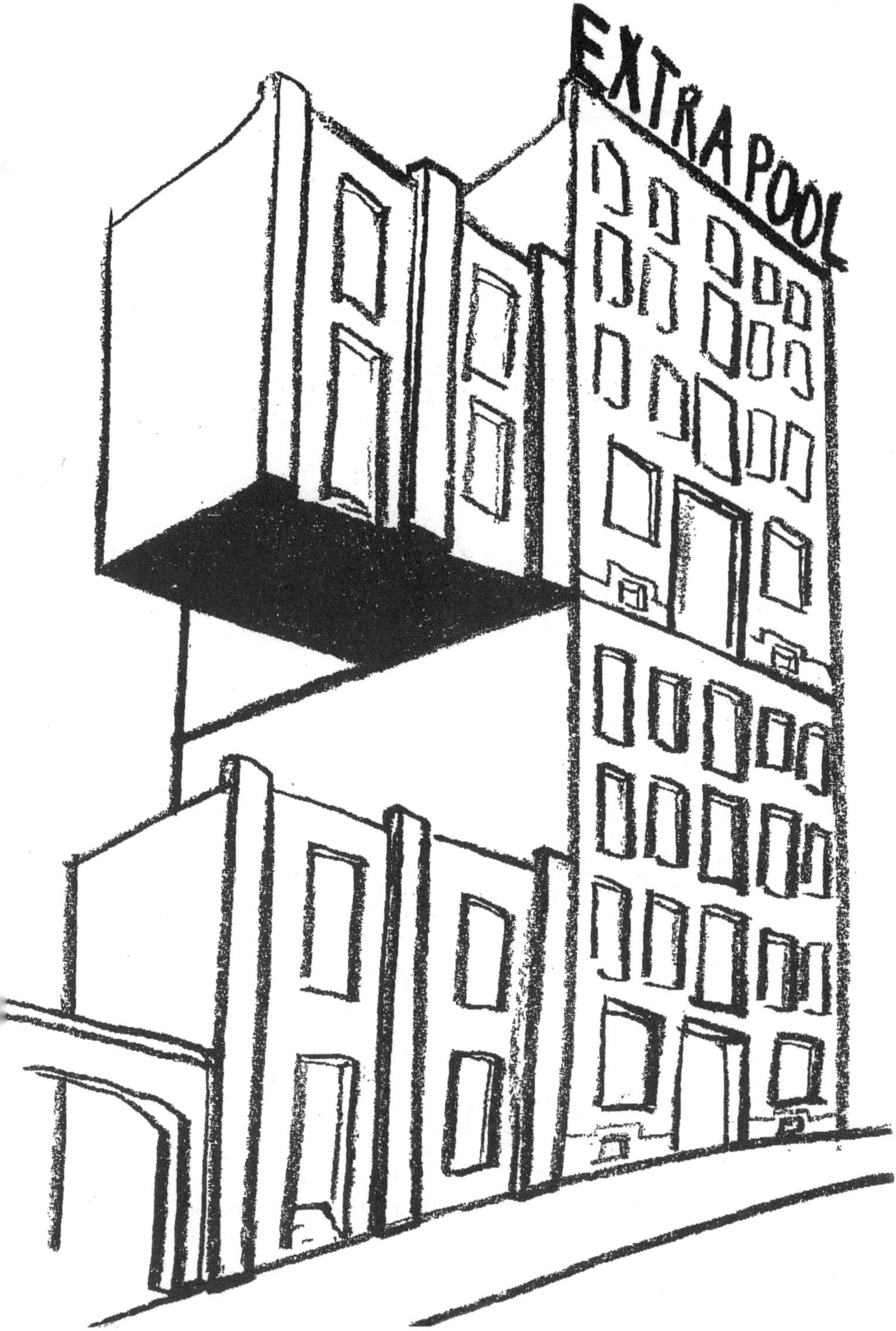
EXTRAPOOL

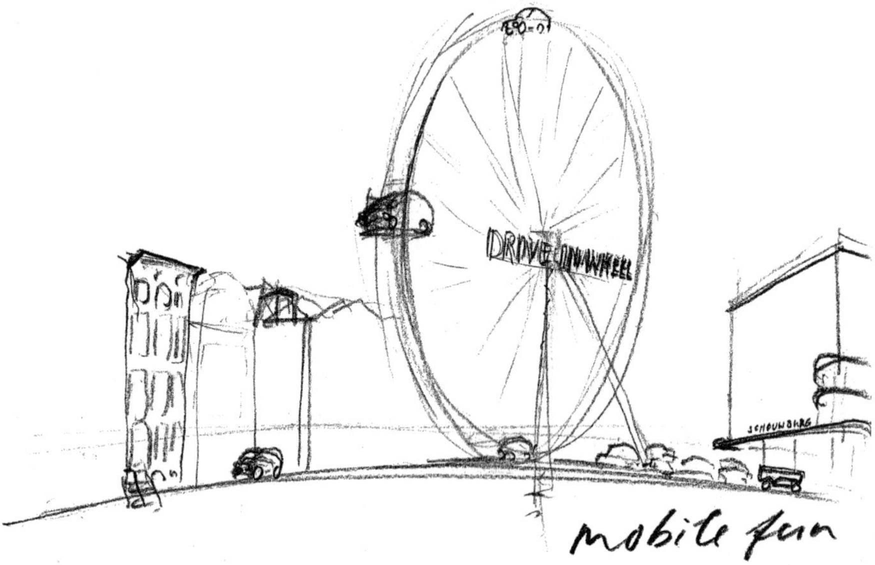
SCHOUWBURG
mobile fun

Discalmer

Every time something is edited with more than one person's work in it
("like violets we are a bunch"—Robin Blaser)
the impulse is to look upon it as an anthology
(ANTHOS LEGERE = flowers gathered)
into some sort of definitive bouquet
All these recent blossoms are fresh
this is not my disclaimer as to their status
(who I *would've* included blah blah blah)
but a DISCALMER—
to stir you/us/them up.
These blossoms
I "picked"
are a snapshot of some vibrant works going on right now
"before and after"
the day everything changed for us
some hidden for a while recently come to light
such as Cecilia Vicuña's early erotic poetry translated here for the first
time in English by Rosa Alcalá. Cecilia Vicuña writes:

> This group of poems, written in Santiago, Chile, in the late sixties, is
> from part of a longer text I called "Diario Estupido" ("Stupid
> Journal"), made out of poems, letters, and other indescribable notes.
> The poems were censored in Chile, and could not be printed until
> much later, when I included a small group of them in my artist book
> *SABORAMI* (Beau Geste Press, UK, 1973).

Jump to the erotic cut-ups of *Cunt-Ups* by Dodie Bellamy, who
writes:

> *Cunt-Ups* is a hermaphroditic salute to William S. Burroughs and
> Kathy Acker . . . Is the cut-up a male form? I've always considered it
> so—needing the violence of a pair of scissors in order to reach non-

linearity. Oddly, even though I've spent up to four hours on each cunt-up, afterwards I cannot recognize them—just like in sex, intense focus and then sensual amnesia.

Stacy Doris's excerpt from her book, *Conference*, though written before September 11, deals with terror and threat, both psychic and actual. I asked her about the plane dialogue and she wrote:

> The Arabic is actually mostly Persian because even though the Flight 900 conversation was in Persian, my book is ostensibly in dialogue with Attar's *Conference of the Birds* (also known as *Language of the Birds*) which I think should have critiqued faith and culture through poetry, but I am not sure if it did. I asked my friend Salar Abdoh, who is an Iranian-born New York espionage writer and terrorism expert, to tell me what the conversation would have been in Persian, and this is mainly transcribed from his letter, except that the repeated and repeated "Twakaltu ala Allah" is in Arabic. That phrase, which means "I believe in Allah," is part of what the investigators made out from the taped cockpit conversation of Flight 900. The rest of the dialogue was also pieced together by investigators, but it appeared in English in *The New York Times*; only the "Twakaltu ala Allah" was given in Arabic. As you probably know, the main language of the non-majority in Afghanistan, the Northern Alliance people, et cetera, is Persian. And the Pashtun majority speaks Pashto which is not Arabic but Indo-European (like Persian). But I was not thinking about that specifically at the time. Anyhow, I think that a lot of poets have written things that somehow foresaw or wanted to dialogue with the possibility of what has happened and is happening . . .

This poetry section was put together before, after, and during the September 11 conflagration and like many acts, felt its influence. I was struck by how the poems I solicited *before* are even read in a different way. For example, Rod Smith's wonderfully abstract "Sandaled" reminds me of the Arabic sandal stepping so into our consciousness.

This is the way it's going to be—beauteous works surfacing from before and after "the event." Maggie Nelson's "The Poem I Was Working on Before September 11" addresses this impulse.

Anselm Berrigan presents a poem "Something like ten million . . ."

written in the same stanzaic form as his forthcoming *Zero Star Hotel* which was written after his stepfather's death, and "is part elegy for him, part its own entity." Now Anselm extends that form into an elegy for everybody. As a correlation, Brian Kim Stefans's excerpt from *The Screens* plays between text blocks and visual screens (both computer and calligraphic), each punctuated by a different set of type symbols used in a structural, concrete manner. Peter Culley's work is at once a cinematic walk through a landscape and through language. Brenda Coultas uncannily, objectively, and obsessively (as if it would make things better) imagines and lists what must go through a person's head as they compose a missing-person poster. Lisa Jarnot's "Self-Portrait" and Cynthia Nelson's swift lyrics are personals that flow with this time. Harryette Mullen's poems "Unacknowledged Legislator" (of the world and of the *unacknowledged* world) and "Headlines" remind us of the unsung place of the poet that we are ALL in as we pass through the daily culture. We need now more than ever to read and respond in language arts to EVERY-THING in this world in all its multiplicitous difficulty.

I hope you enjoy reading these multidisciplinary, multi-genre, multigenerational, multiply influenced poetic works.

Lee Ann Brown
New York City
October 22, 2001

Unacknowledged Legislator

Harryette Mullen

After singing the final page
the poet passes out
ceremonial pens.

As the poem is sighed into law
rules to be made are broken
and broken rules amended.

When the archival papers
are all singed in blood
the poet's meter expires.

Headlines

Harryette Mullen

1. Fired cook was deranged.
2. Bald-headed woman's distressed.
3. Flypaper gets inspected.
4. Trial lawyer's profession distorted.
5. Balloonist disgusted, round-the-world trip falls flat.
6. Kiwis, these birds are unflappable.
7. Obese sheep distended.
8. Madonna disguised in convent.
9. Jockey to be debriefed shortly.
10. Hollywood delighted to conserve power.

Bumper to Bumper

Harryette Mullen

I'd rather be at the beach. I'd rather beat each ache. I'd rather be a
dirty blond than a clean-cut brunet. If I had to choose between being
smarter or richer, I'd rather have the money because I'm smart enough
already.

I'd rather not think about it. I'd rather not go into that. I voted
but I'd rather not say which one I punched. I'd rather switch than
fight. I trust my psychic friend over Dan Rather.

I'm stuck in traffic when I'd rather be surfing. My other car is the
Metro, *mi otro carro es el Metro*. I'd rather drive than walk. I'd
rather work than starve. I'd rather drink unfiltered tap water and
sleep on a lumpy futon than live anywhere else in this godforsaken
world.

Sandaled

Rod Smith

I love weasel ball. I love the soft night of skulls.
Take me to your creation. Take me to the fender
of rain behind the wall of immaterial vitality. O
distant beam. O resnowed lit til of sneeze. Let
the angel of light show all that die the shook
leanings of salves & pulsation. Let summer's
prospectus trace out a wake of amorous globes.
Raptor world Raptor knight
The potatoes pivot, knought in the grieving, knought
in the round. Let this governed motioning constant
abutt me blank a plausible rainbow of I love.

Flight
from *Conference*

Stacy Doris

BELBEL: To master living with obsession is life and death but also generation: how your breathing becomes substitution. You're a tambourine now. Follow me.

When I love in the act and nowhere else, I am not my body, and the act may be flight. Your limbs are tools. Trade yourself in. Become merely that or which I am; you are: no self. A basic truth:

BELBEL: Gravity delivers stones. Cliffs deliver what flies. Culture delivers men as messages, each the same drab path's ambassador. Who needs that? Ascent by magnet:

Where you are the hollow of my hollow, where nowhere is where, I'm drawn or torn in, where drab is its most foreign practice. Because if the sky hollows you, my hollow, is it an architecture after all? Thus deception, breathing in no and in where at once, thus living in division, being as both bird and drab, here and there. This wrenches the hollow. Such is what I'd aspire back to, bomb or balm. Back to my jar.

So my friend sets out for a jungle, which separates me from her. "In the calendar of the long count," says my friend, "the years go in various lengths: 144,000, then 7,200, then 360, then 20, then one days. Nobody knows what determined these years."

BELBEL: Deception would dictate: "I am if I go/If I don't go I'm not," where going is a wave. However, if I go, I am or am not, and if I don't go, the same. That is why **B**'s living makes a life for you, endlessly, else-where, nearly always. Why you must and will be my sacrifice, despite you.

I've ruined everything/To save this practice of a Royalty contem-plated through selves, and the high quality of relations and efforts it founds. With the endless end of showing a primacy of **B** over bird, the drab declares or preaches **B**, but in flight, there's a problem, since air's a bundling bundle of quantities. It blinds and blocks the way to any clarity, as logic is untranslatable to feeling. The role of each is enrichment, which escapes us or you.

BELBEL: You will give your life for what you have or are; you dissolve thus.

Because **B** is flight, not exposition, we (or birds) hollow **B** in us, then rage at drab inaction. We (or birds) neglecting flight, survive, which is pure drowning or deception, as to admit, even separate from my friend, the sun's setting. Thus flight received a true or false name of sacrifice.

Sacrifice was no amputation or penance, but rather plain move-ment. Thus an act. Act or protest. To sacrifice yourself to breath is belief or embellishment, making of air an unending domain. Is defeat meaning love. Domain is a sum of giving, not of givens. Sacrifice trapped in the hollow of my or birds' hollows. Due to pure expression, thus and from it (cedar's after) did I turn your life away from knowing to just affirming, which is sacrifice. You or I vanish thus (after's cedar). Then the sun . . . what I said. My mistake was in replacing the assortment of birds for **B**. Thus something—not nothing—collective installed, meaning perhaps moral or inanimate. And in explaining why birds should be the sacrifice of **B**, but unable to exact **B**'s sacrifice to birds, any definition fails from now on. This, in acts of memory, you forget, which, separating me or us from fear, is our magnitude.

I or birds glide, then, without efficient method, from **B** to temerity, and in multiplication. A voided vocable, then, applied to each song, thus each cancels other, and nowhere does not accrue in its mere accumulation. Where each is the same, each day. So there are days, meaning hollows. The tale of how speaking begot forgetting. Tale of how **B** tripped from liberty to license of variable degrees, thus a staircase perhaps.

Thus **B** may be lost. Good riddance or farewell.

(Flight 990)

1:57 CO-PILOT: Twakaltu ala Allah.
0:48 CO-PILOT: Twakaltu ala Allah.
0:39 CO-PILOT: Twakaltu ala Allah.
0:38 CO-PILOT: Twakaltu ala Allah.
0:36 CO-PILOT: Twakaltu ala Allah.
0:35 CO-PILOT: Twakaltu ala Allah.
0:34 CO-PILOT: Twakaltu ala Allah.
0:32 CO-PILOT: Twakaltu ala Allah.
0:31 CO-PILOT: Twakaltu ala Allah.

0:30 PILOT: Che khabare? Che khabare?

0:29 CO-PILOT: Twakaltu ala Allah.
0:28 CO-PILOT: Twakaltu ala Allah.

0:28 PILOT: Che khabare?

0:21 PILOT: Che khabare, Gamil? Che khabare?

0:20 PILOT: Een chiye? Een chiye? Motor o khaamoosh kardi?

0:10 PILOT: Boro motor o khaamoosh kon.

0:07 CO-PILOT: Khaamooshe.

0:05 PILOT: Bekesh.

0:05 PILOT: Baa man bekesh.
0:05 PILOT: Baa man bekesh.
0:05 PILOT: Baa man bekesh.
0:05 PILOT: Baa man bekesh.

The Brilliance of Orifices

Cecilia Vicuña

In fact, I can tell you a story
talk about my boyfriend sweet brick
of Indian skin and volcanic design
with seven craters, each
having their own characteristics
For example, one has lips
and is the patience crater
the most humorous and witty
In addition, from it comes my boyfriend's
poetry and basic delight
There are two craters however
from which nothing comes, instead
things enter
they are called ENTRANCES FOR MUSIC
and are somewhat wrinkled
Crudely known as ears
they are the softest love devices
my boyfriend never cleans them for fear
he might dull or scratch them,
the way one might damage a record
thus ending a fountain of miracles
The last two craters not only allow things
to exit, but also to enter
They cover a moist organ,
and go FOOZ FOOZ when functioning
To them we owe the grace of aromas
and mustiness

OPEN CITY

That is why they are called awakeners
or INDEXES OF SENSITIVITY
and he who has well-developed ones
is fortunate
and they call my boyfriend LUCKY FORTUNATO
Even though his name is Claudio

Mother of Pearl

Cecilia Vicuña

I started collecting tiny nacre shells
fragmented and turning to dust.
Gathering the bits of air
between them was tough.
I was able to fill two rooms
with shells
blue and dark green
without repeating
one form
one small piece
one air.
All were sleeping
a white vagueness
dampened them.

The Anatomy of Paper

Cecilia Vicuña

The strange thing is that the sheet
stood on its own
without an erect
beam backing it up.
This surprised me
in the same way
that your sex
has no bone
yet it is harder
than a knee
which has various bones,
five or six I believe.

Three poems translated from the Spanish by Rosa Alcalá.

From **Cunt-Ups**

Dodie Bellamy

Seventeen

We felt for one another, coursing through the photographs, within range within everywhere, and I knew it was you, your navel or vagina because this is what my cock looks like. But I'm still licking your membrane, filled with some semi-fluid substance. You're an eminent gynecologist and you've lobotomized your cunt. I've agreed to run my tongue along your scar. I slide a portion of my substance into your vagina, this manifests as love, connecting us, and blood rolls out to our sides in luminous threads. The substance left me (unintentionally), can I still take you sometimes, physically, can we still cuddle and fuck? Can we fuck too? I manifest in front of you, unzipping your pants, you should be happy when you come because my little pointed tongue with its red tip can lay our burdens at the door. And I can't keep your pussy off my dick. Now don't degenerate into a phantasm, Puppy. Dear Fuck Slug. Dear Fuck Instrument through which one can express us. In either case we are cranberry. Desire for you is dripping out, a dispiriting state of affairs. Sweet Psyche can I suck your nipples? Do you like to move it? I threw my mass upon the table, vulnerable, my breast for instance and all my orifices, and then my lips close around the head of your cock. Do you wanna fuck my brains out, do you wanna make my pineal gland come? Suppressed by light, the grand climax is reached. Honey, don't make me so fucking horny, it all dissolves, and we'll go straight down, ectoplasm leaking from your body, your tits upwards towards faces so you can be visible, a soft resilient mass. I skin you alive like a fucking rabbit. I show you the photographs and they're wet. I'm huffing as I'm trying to pack a considerable punch, I'm just going to think about it throughout, expelling a cloudy medium, faintly this time like we're teenagers. I'm kissing you, emerging like a baby in fluid, kneeling between your legs, my cock extracted from your sensitive body, my head moving back and forth, my lips a veil of splendor, our hearts cocked, my eyes closed like a blind mole. What an ecstasy of joy, seeing you press yourself up against me. Give us some rest, aid us to wipe it away. I clean you with my tongues, I'm licking your body wetter until your body looks shiny with desire. Just so, the spirits are in control, they want you to move through me. All this is baffling, your left hand down there with the spirits still controlling the marks on the insides of my scrotum. I'm reaching for you. Plasm is exuded from my legs and there's a landslide along my clit, which is responsive to light. I'm rubbing my cock up against you, intensified by darkness. No language will ever fit, no language will give light to the mysteries of my overwhelming need to tell you that I want.

Eighteen

A kind of liquid jelly is dripping all over me. Your cunt organizes itself into the shape of a face, your tongue was in convulsions, thrusting, jerking, I started to move, and you told me what your hands were like. Your clit likes someone in orgasm, feel my wet tongue in your cave, your cunt is happy to hear that the young man's activity will get red. Your nipples bleed because of my ejaculations, the substance, whatever it is, goes straight to my brain. Your pussy is mine mine mine. Cold shocks cause an irreversible spilling out of my pussy and it's harder to swallow with your broken tongue, you're all red. Your limbs could be so successful they looked real, felt real, and smelled real, always pushing my clit. My hand clings to your clit like a barnacle, honey. Take me, the love-fuck of the century, you're naked. Looking for sustenance your cock swayed and throbbed. Naked your whole body is a kind of light: I investigated it early in this century: it burned trying to hide someone. We're really fucking now, all we had has fallen into one big cunt, especially my brain, you called it death, but it is just a step in enabling my come. You've got specially made clothes on, understanding the truth, I'm sowing my seeds, you're completely at my

Dodie Bellamy

mercy, nervous as I watch you tonight. Does it feel good that way? Yes I can be consumed. I'm thinking of you, I bet you have the cutest sledge-hammer, bet you could break the bones up inside of me, slamming into me. I can come just in the woods. You make sounds like broken bubbles, I can see you now, fucking body parts, I can taste you now, dissolving on my tongue. I can see your cunt was the biceps. I can't fuck donuts, can't stand waiting to sniff your come soaked underwear. Apparently they are missing and I cannot find your asshole. I clean the funk from my apart-ment, I scraped up the pus from our wounds and the come I hadn't eaten and flushed them down the toilet, the jungle. I did come, but my cock didn't pose for you, I gave you a drink and then my love in an electrified sea. I didn't know your skin was acid, it skinned my entire voice. I want to suck them like a baby and subsequently to dispose my body in the still of your cunt. I don't know how you feel when I strangle you, I don't think my clit liked the black strap, leather type, that you pulled out of the blue, it made me wonder if you were.

"Something like ten million . . ."

Anselm Berrigan

OPEN CITY

Something like ten million
Land mines in the papers
Land born to die on
Bombed on delay
This time around
Soft collateral ghosts
Claim space for
A broader application
Of how deep the
Intelligence failure runs

all high all the time
the fabric of business
continues, unwilling
to pretend I'm not
scared, find myself
leading loaded conversations
about how not to cave
into some elemental
fear, the inability
to live with anyone

In Union Square last
Night, people running
The United Homeless
Organization estimated
One hundred homeless lost
Unrecorded dust
As of September 11
Grief can't be told
When to stop speaking
How to behave or

spent night sounds like
someone I am not
and that hoax of a self
is going to be pushed
night after night into
the mind's deepest recesses
of terror. Go to symbol
embrace. Transient grief
medium ready to jump
on any feeling talking

Who to blame.
It's a kind of sight
Even as the same
Basic male facial types
Con us into nationalism
Masked as love of country
Time and time again
But that's a surface.
Underneath, ordinary
Civilians have been

or questioning itself
out of unity. I
don't see how living
our former lives
constitutes a rational
defense, gas in the
throat as normal
New York City condition
portal-filled realities
& rhapsodies notwithstanding

Anselm Berrigan

Massacred repeatedly
All along, all over
The planet with some
Lying definition of freedom
Or god served as justification
An unfiltered, open
Manifestation of feeling
For thousands of lives
Erased in seconds
Is a reality this city

Poker face back on
When we've barely
Begun to recognize
The number of dead.
Billionaires shoot
Their guns with god
Or law as license
Babbling about nation
Building, history's
Tripwire, a longer

Shall fear no evil—
For I am a lot more
Insane than
This Valley."
Trapped
Tricked
In mourning
Under attack
All at once
Better make

is capable of sustaining
see evidence of that
every day now
not the most people
ever murdered at once
but by far the most
witnesses: imaginations
subject to scripted acts
of cruelty televised eternally
I don't want to put my

duration between the
stumble and its crippling
explosion. Their credo
something like my
father's take on lines
our cowboy Prez
dropped on us:
"Yea, though I walk
through the Valley of
the Shadow of Death, I

room for each
grief letting
me see what
lines and
lies
not to take,
and how,
moment
by moment
to be.

Two Pages from The Screens

Brian Kim Stefans

ot's idea of "evil" (Baudelaire). The poetry of bulk ↔ Arid extra dry. Ambience ↔ The speaking subject. Boy those Asians are smart ↔ Boy those Asians are dumb. The Who ↔ The Beatles. Helen Keller/Arakawa ↔ Anthony Hecht/Yasusada. The standard ↔ The non-standard. Cult of speed (Bruce Andrews) ↔ Cult of slowness (Jennifer Moxley). Utopia (punk) ↔ Fatalism (grunge). Fashion ↔ Ethics. Extreme ↔ Center. Pragmatism (American) ↔ Catholicism (French). Gertrude Stein ↔ Ezra Pound. Steve McCaffery ↔ Ezra Pound. John Cage ↔ Ezra Pound. John Cage ↔ Ian Hamilton Finlay. Tall and skinny (variable foot) ↔ Short and fat (iambic pentameter). Cadence (vowels) ↔ Percussion (consonants). A cabal of malcontents ↔ A stable of professionals. Horizontal (social) ↔ Vertical (private). Kevin Davies ↔ Ange Mlinko. Soliloquy ↔ Dialogue. A poetics of information ↔ A poetics of achievement. The large canvas (*I Don't Have Any Paper So Shut Up, or Social Romanticism*). ↔ The small canvas (*The Collected Poems of Robert Creeley*). Monotheism ↔ Polytheism. Collage ↔ Plein air. Stone ↔ Paper. Paper ↔ Screen. Screen ↔ Garden. Literary tradition (Jennifer Moxley) ↔ Literary lineage (Robert Fitterman). Originality / improvisation (Tim Davis) ↔ Mastery / imitation (Miles Champion). Homage ↔ Insult. West coast (slow, meditative, attractive coloration, subtle changes in the weather) ↔ East coast (fast, schizophrenic, threatening coloration, profound changes in the weather). Rockstar (Jim Morrison) ↔ Wallflower (Joseph Cornell). Exhibitionist ↔ Virtuoso. Reading ↔ Parsing. Beauty ↔ Experience. A human-scale Thomas Pynchon ↔ A cosmic-scale Robbe-Grillet. Australia ↔ Canada. Form ↔ Flux. Critics who can write poetry ↔ Critics who can't write poetry. Edmund Berrigan ↔ Anselm Berrigan. Memory through madeleines (Marcel Proust) ↔ Experience through chickens (William Carlos Williams). Debut volume (forgotten) ↔ Posthumous volume (remembered). The language of birds ↔ The language of priests. Juve-

ing. | A calculated instance (among distrust): lost in *Europe.* | We thought it was Dutch: it was *Flemish.* | As in: where to go *next.* | Running out of drink, then: where is the *fountain.* | Trying: to angle the *light.* | Grossly spiritual, she takes a number: she is *waiting.* | Productive backslide: thinking back to *terms.* | I am here: you are *there.* | How many times have you been there: and I've *choked.* | A sliver of counter-honesty: spicy *discussion.* | Nonetheless, remembering: *remembering.* | The crowd was fucked: *fucked.* | Bouncing a ball: waiting for the next *line.* | Moment by the moment, the web was built: *falters.* | Later: taking a *test.* | That writer who wrote of love and fame: that writer who *died.* | Production ceased: of *course.* | Making noises with the pen: scratch, *tap.* | And when she turns to me: forgetting *amnesty.* | The life gets better, but the writing: *worse.* | Dialing up: tuning (getting) *out.* | Indecision is insufferable: then, the *rain.* | When the masculine forecloses: athletic *poem.* | A drop: then, *sound.* | Trying: negotiating a *wave.* | Thinking it was Cage, knowing finally: *Eno.* | Pacing back and forth, smoking, fidgeting: *behavior.* | Cars on the highway: moving forth into *adventure.* | When it bleeds: *satire.* | Scanning the crowd for the familiar: *faces.* | Two words together that make a dull story: *theory.* | Crying: public *address.* | Anticipating: public *demonstrations.* | When the polls close: catharsis of the new *naive.* | On the streets, garbage, dust: *sediment.* | I think: I have *invented.* | Blowing the nose into an ashtray: improbable *dissent.* | The pathology of getting it wrong: *dada.* | Tryng to circulate among nuance: flexing the *Jamesian.* | And when the table cleared, and the conversation ceased: my *family.* | Birds warble: *morning.* | Cheap jokes and laughing gas: *community.* | The image profoundly dithers: the site is *ugly.* | When the chips are finally counted: *pragmatism.* | No longer: puppet of *stars.* | No longer: victim of the *contiguous.* | No longer: angling to be a stable *critic.* | After a failure of short-term memory: renew the *streets.* | Every temp its turn: every type its *torque.* | Sort of: being there, or being *awake.* | These emis-

Self-Portrait

Lisa Jarnot

Fifty-seven dollars and the four
cents I left on the desk in room 118,
not much else a half a cup of tea,
unfinished books, some phone
numbers, the Wolf Man, tenacity,
one cat, at home in Brooklyn
with the spiders and also 7th
Avenue, the basement of Macy's,
the L train, the hello lady at
the Korean market on 14th
Street, hardly any smoking of pot,
was thrown out of the Charleston,
have a wheelie-cart for my luggage,
two tranquilizers, four Prozac,
minor elk viewing, movie stardom,
and the greatest waves of
happiness this sixth day of July.

go ahead and sing your weird arias

Cynthia Nelson

thirsty don't wanna buy snapple lemonade ghost beverage
from the train station café try a vending machine but when you
push coke all that falls out is too many hot dogs
then slowly after that falls too many cokes
so you go down to the bottoms, to a fish fry
get sexed up by a frog woman, get girlfriended
by that time they're out of fish and salad
and the line's too long, your clothes are too
hanging off of you in weird areas
go ahead and sing
your public thirst

the adoration piles of spring

Cynthia Nelson

i've come to catch the feeling between
the sleeves of february & the halters of summer
the mothers in letters & the drips of omniscience
a day of steerage, west as in village
home as in F train
weekend as in the shattering release
of tentatively knowing what's owed
wrapping hands around tawny brown bags
blackbirds splashing in a puddle
all assignments are in, installations installed
it is needing to be written by the daily white grime

i almost get killed

Cynthia Nelson

i am running outside of a rock club.
there is an original noise inside me. i smell
like a rock club. i smell smoke. lying on a bed
has made me slower. so i'm starting to run. the
engine barks. the engine barks at me. the beautiful
white chalk. flashing impenetrable. making a
whack sound. running from the yellow beetle. falling
for the next nine yards. drowning in the curb. a four-point
landing. watch me hop up unscathed. only skinners.
a hole in white tights. then watery tears. can't keep it
together. whore.

House Is a Feeling
for Daphne

Peter Culley

Beneath the cobblestones, the beach
—Situationist International

syntax of place divulges the outward
—Ted Pearson

House is a feeling.

A thing
    to which other things are added.

    120 beats per minute give or take—

A point where concrete foundations

gravel off into fields, lift
    over tracks
hedges, trellis, white

shutters, trails off hung window limp
yellow lace like smoke, half-basements

    asbestos green grid upturned

OPEN CITY

flaking chainlink submerged in
deadly unreachable blackberry. Pipe tobacco
smell of new hay, futz

    of weekday stretchers
    double Income
    rural types, *rentiers,*
    pensionnaires
    lacking only ruffles

blinkered petting
    as if to
rub up against it
were sufficient—

a llama peering through
the towering fennel
emits a hard sharp buzz
over its hinged lower teeth
but cannot otherwise
disguise its interest

    A certain hitch
a flatted fifth
and then it's as if
you're singing:

    Mr. Fingers
bangs a skillet
against a retaining wall
and they are all retaining walls,

Peter Culley

airlessly pressing
his hard thumb
on my reddened thorax—

  south of that you
might as well float away
if transfer you seek,
transfusion
like steam off a workshop roof

  A long mixed block of Milton
  flat a little shiny, overhung
  granite cladded, blasted smooth
  but then laterally
  scored and scratched
  as if by cats,
  grain elevator, wild garden
  overspill, holly welt,
  shredded bales of wire
  padlocked lumberyard—

  The reign of
  piety and iron
  concluded:

a flattened fork (he argues)
a business card from a Honda dealer (speaks)
a broad bright yellow leaf (a map)
creased where the tide broke (foxed)
a sedimentary reversal

  Divided it and then
  divided it again

OPEN CITY

a rolling snare
a drop
divided kick, then split
divide it again
and then oh up
from the engine room
from the inside
from the outside

Oh monumentalising beam!
  Refulgent 303!
On waves and waves of filtered pink
  carpet this afternoon!

By the South Gate
  the north advances
dollar store early birds prop
  no frontage no street corner no size
surfs up cabinets of
  yellowish dust
they seen it was only
  in the space it took
Ives to pan the cortège
  with an archival flicker:

a ragged line that ran across the windowsill
red Topaz umbrella lowering
palm leaves with a damp cloth
everything south of the fold
muffled unanswered
muted stanchion
resurfaced spongiform roadway
gives way to a park

about eighteen foot square
    all gate

a parting gift
    from a beloved creditor
    with an unsurprisable mind;

a client state
    addressed from a thinking cloud

reversals gleam
like dew on an unmown lawn—

speech or its opposite
flutters the blinds
at the moment of sleep—

The Poem I Was Working on Before September 11, 2001

Maggie Nelson

Say something awful, say
"She leaned on the fork"

Say something beautiful, say
"Eyes smudged with soft kohl"

Now lead the way under
the spiders, yes under the spiders

where a bad woman rules. Glassy
white eggs in a wrought-iron

grid—she almost goes through
with it. Engulfed in a perfect

day, the pressure lifts—
urban life is OK as long as

there is still wind, something new
to breathe, though do you want

to know what that strange smell is
Well I'll tell you it's the fumigation

of the lizards in the subway system,
KEEP CLEAR, DO NOT INHALE.

OPEN CITY

O you're so gullible. But can I breathe here—where?—
in this tiny circle, where the homunculus

is hopping on the gamelan and playing
the song of joyful death—just think

about that. Say something nice, say
"Your sexiness is necessarily an aporia,

but that just means nothing can ever
demolish it." Now that we're grown up

and have no willpower (of all things!)
The absurdity is I hope this will never, ever end—

not the banging on the can, not the dark brown liquid
in the blue glass. I love it here, on Earth—I don't care a fig

for what comes next, which is exactly what
the suicide bomber said of the Israelis he killed yesterday

at the discotheque. There is something bestial
in me, it wants to be drunk on saliva, and

there is something ugly about me, which has to do
with my fear of dying of hives. But above all

there is something very lovely about today,
the day I wandered beneath a great spider

and the city opened itself up as if to apologize
for its heat and changing ways.

Maggie Nelson

Don't sit there slobbering all over
the thermometer! The least you could do

is try to capture an enigma with an image,
or don't sweat it—out West my mother

is fondling the stone bellies of the Three Graces.
She waters everything at night now, she is

the night gardener, she goes out with a flashlight
and looks for insects doing their deeds. Looks

for all that oozes underneath. Yesterday I saw
a man burn a strip of skin off his arm—

he just threw the skin in the trash
and for a moment we all stood there, staring

at the bright white streak on his arm. It didn't look like
anything. Then the red blood started to perk up

around the edges, it was quite eerie and beautiful,
it was the skin under the skin, it was

the flesh. Our flesh is often so red
in the photos that get taken of us, and I admit

that something about life overheats me, but nothing like
the teenager who overdosed on Ecstasy and was found

on her kitchen floor with a body temperature of 104 degrees.
I saw it on the News, the News whose job it is to scare me.

OPEN CITY

It would seem by such a lead story that
these are decadent and peaceful times, but there is

much else. But the rest doesn't count. The bottom half
always drops out, as George W. dines along the Venice canal.

But today—just today—I felt new for the first time this century—
no one noticed me—I was unsexed!—I stood

in front of *Les Demoiselles d' Avignon*;
I could take it or leave it. I read Dr. Williams

in the park, he says the sun parts the clouds
like labia (I guess he would know). Looking up

from my book I became momentarily afraid
of the polar situations that may arise between us,

but then I let it all go. I'm tired of small dry things.
I want to nestle into the clammy crack

between conscience and id—speaking of which,
I'm so glad you turned me on to donut peaches—

they will taste like this summer until
they taste like next summer, but why

think about that yet? You never let me see you naked
but when you do it is like a rain of almonds, your soft spots

smell so tart and floral, and you don't pull me into you often
but when you do you pull me into you. All of this

is worth fighting for. We may be called upon
to do so, in which case there will be no more Ovaltine,

no therapy, no crackers. Praying is just thinking
about nothing, or trying not to think about

the lines of cows, their fat nipples squeezed
into the machines. (I'm surprised the milk

still comes out!) Through a hole in my head I imagine
my brain seeping out, in shell-pink ribbons

as the village moderates itself into night:
bottles are getting recycled, objects are left behind

in moving vehicles, people remove their earrings and war paint
and get ready to sleep. Tomorrow is Saturday,

and the city will rise. There could be a planet out there
whose inhabitants are watching our demise, but enough

already about the living dead! There may be
neither space nor time in the space and time

in which I love you, and thus our love
will remain iridescent forever, and have only

as much sternness as the universe has to offer
(which may or may not be much). There *is* a world

that I think, but it is not different from this one.
The great spider and her shadow, the clouds

moving across the mirrored Cineplex—they're real, too.

To Write It Down

Brenda Coultas

To write their names, to print their names in letters large enough to be seen from a distance, to catch someone's eye. To talk about their tattoos or other identification marks, to talk about height and hair and skin color. To find a photograph that someone, a stranger, could recognize them from. To talk about the floor they worked on or the firm they worked for, the last phone call, the last words they spoke, to say "Take care of my children" to say "I love you" or to say "The room is full of smoke."

To make a poster about it, to make a poster in case someone should see them or so that the world sees them and calls, they might be anywhere, traumatized, unrecognizable, naked—even just to recognize a leg or arm or tooth.

To place it in a public place where no one could miss it. On the street at eye level, in a window, on a pole, on the mailbox, on a wall, or in a public park. If there is no place to put it then make a place, others will come and leave flowers and candles. And someone will be by to keep the candles lit, someone will water the flowers, and someone will tidy it up.

To describe a personality, to talk about what they liked to do, to talk about whether they liked to cook or not, or what books they liked to read, to write down in public the movies they enjoyed, to write down if they liked NYC or if they liked their job or if they were fulfilled. Did they like sports? Did they practice a certain religious faith? Is there something you could say to make them come alive for us? Some singular trait of individuality or even normalcy?

Be sure to say if they were parents or single or married or divorced. Or write down who is waiting to hear, who is missing them, to write down your cell phone and your home phone numbers. Be sure to write down your name so if someone or anyone calls they know who they are speaking to. If the missing has children be sure to include a photograph of them because then strangers will be more likely to read your poster.

To you the reader
Be sure to carry a rose to a firehouse
To carry a lit candle down the street
To hang a banner
To wear a ribbon,
To visit a hospital
To walk by the wall
To read the wall
Then to follow a plume of smoke as close as possible to the source.

Paintings, 1977–1987

René Daniëls

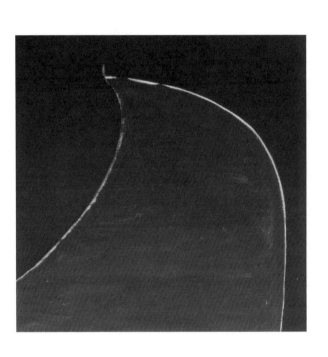

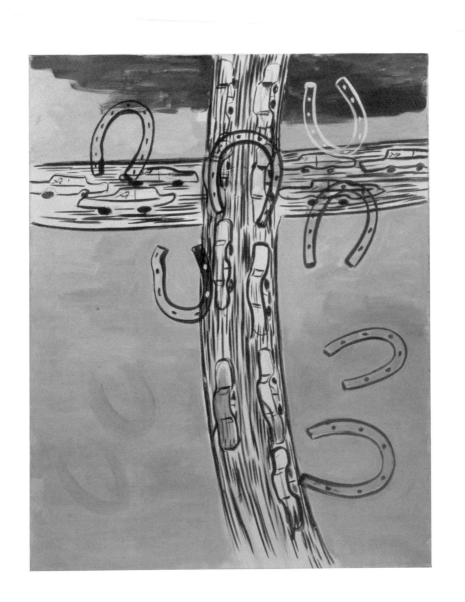

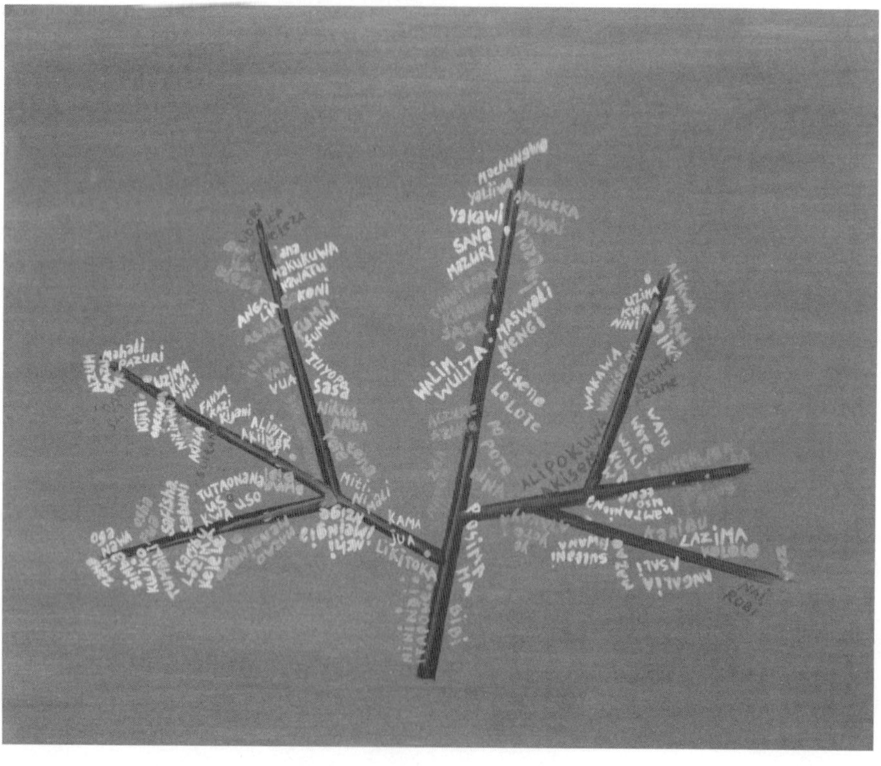

yaliiva
yakawi
SANA
MAZURI
MASWALI
MENGI
WALIM
WULIZA
LOLOTE
NAKUKUWA
KONI
ANGA
TUMIA
VUA
sasa
mahali
PAZURI
UZIMA
KWA
NINI
FANYA
KAZI
Kijani
TUTAONANA
USO
KAMA
JUA
LIKITOKA
WAKAWA
VATU
LAZIMA
ASALI
ANGALIA
NAI
ROBI

Sumerian Economics

Hakim Bey

PUBLIC SECRET: EVERYONE KNOWS BUT NO ONE SPEAKS. Another kind of public secret: the fact is published but no one pays attention.

A cuneiform tablet called *The Sumerian King List* states that "kingship first descended from heaven in the city of Eridu," in the south of Sumer. Mesopotamians believed Eridu the oldest city in the world, and modern archaeology confirms the myth. Eridu was founded about 5000 B.C. and disappeared under the sand around the time of Christ.

Eridu's god Enki (a kind of Neptune and Hermes combined) had a ziggurat where fish were sacrificed. He owned the *ME*, the fifty-one principles of civilization. The first king, named Staghorn, probably ruled as Enki's high priest. After some centuries came the Flood, and kingship had to descend from heaven again, this time in Uruk and Ur. Gilgamesh now appears on the list. The Flood actually occurred; Sir Leonard Wooley saw the thick layer of silt at Ur between two inhabited strata.

Bishop Ussher once calculated according to the Bible that the world was created on October 19, 4004 B.C. at nine o'clock in the morning. This makes no Darwinian sense, but provides a good date for the founding of the Sumerian state, which certainly created a new world. Abraham came from Ur of the Chaldees; Genesis owes much to the *Enuma Elish* (Mesopotamian Creation Myth). Our only text is late Babylonian but obviously based on a lost Sumerian original.

Marduk the wargod of Babylon has apparently been pasted over a series of earlier figures beginning with Enki.

Before the creation of the world as we know it a family of deities held sway. Chief among them at the time, Tiamat (a typical avatar of the universal Neolithic earth goddess) described by the text as a dragon or serpent, rules a brood of monsters and dallies with her "Consort" (high priest) Kingu, an effeminate Tammuz/Adonis prototype. The youngest gods are dissatisfied with her reign; they are "noisy," and Tiamat (the text claims) wants to destroy them because their noise disturbs her slothful slumber. In truth the young gods are simply fed up with doing all the shit work themselves because they are not "humans" yet. The gods want Progress. They elect Marduk their king and declare war on Tiamat.

A gruesome battle ensues. Marduk triumphs. He kills Tiamat and slices her body lengthwise in two. He separates the halves with a mighty ripping heave. One half becomes sky above, the other earth below.

Then he kills Kingu and chops his body up into gobs and gobbets. The gods mix the bloody mess with mud and mold little figurines. Thus humans are created as robots of the gods. The poem ends with a triumphalist paean to Marduk, new king of heaven.

Clearly the Neolithic is over. City god, wargod, metal god vs. country goddess, lazy goddess, garden goddess. The creation of the world equals the creation of civilization, separation, hierarchy, masters and slaves, above and below. Ziggurat and pyramid symbolize the new shape of life.

Combining *Enuma elish* and the *King List* we get an explosive secret document about the origin of civilization not as gradual evolution toward inevitable future, but as violent coup, conspiratorial overthrow of primordial rough egalitarian Stone Age society by a crew of black-magic cult cannibals. (Human sacrifice first appears in the archaeological record at Ur III. Similar grisly phenomenon in the first few Egyptian dynasties.)

About 3100 writing was invented at Uruk. Apparently you can witness the moment in the strata: one layer no writing, next layer writing. Of course writing has a prehistory (like the State). From ancient times a system of accounting had grown up based on the little clay counters in the shapes of commodities (hides, jars of oil, bars of metal, et cetera) Also glyphic seals had been invented with images used heraldically to designate the seals' owners. Counters and seals were pressed into slabs of wet clay and the records were held in Temple archives—probably records of debts owed to the Temple. (In the Neolithic the temples no doubt served as redistribution centers. In the Bronze Age they began to function as banks.)

As I picture it the invention of real writing took place within a single brilliant family of temple archivists over three or four generations, say a century. The counters were discarded and a reed stylus was used to impress signs in clay, based on the shapes of the old counters, and with further pictograms imitated from the seals. Numbering was easily compacted from rows of counters to number signs. The real breakthrough came with the flash that certain pictographs could be used with their sound divorced from their meaning and recombined to "spell" other words (especially abstractions). Integrating the two systems proved cumbersome, but maybe the sly scribes considered this an advantage. Writing needed to be difficult because it was a mystery revealed by gods and a monopoly of the New Class of scribes. Aristocrats rarely learned to read and write—a matter for mere bureaucrats. But writing provided the key to state expansion by separating sound from meaning, speaker from hearer, and sight from other senses. Writing as separation both mirrors and reenforces separation as "written," as fate. Action-at-a-distance (including distance of time) constitutes the magic of the state, the nervous system of control. Writing *is* and *represents* the new Creation ideology. It wipes out the oral tradition of the Stone Age and erases the collective memory of a time before hierarchy. In the text we have always been slaves.

By combining image and word in single memes or hieroglyphs the scribes of Uruk (and a few years later the pre-dynastic scribes of Egypt) created a magical system. According to a late syncretistic Greco-Egyptian myth, when Hermes-Thoth invents writing he boasts to his father Zeus that humans now never need forget anything ever again. Zeus replies, "On the contrary my son, now they'll forget *everything*." Zeus discerned the occult purpose of the text, the forgetfulness of the oral/aural, the false memory of the text, indeed the *lost* text. He sensed a void where others saw only a plenum of information. But this void is the *telos* of writing.

Writing begins as a method of controlling debt owed to the Temple, debt as yet another form of absence. When full-blown economic texts appear a few strata later we find ourselves already immersed in a complex economic world based on debt, interest, compound interest, debt peonage as well as outright slavery, rents, leases, private and public forms of property, long-distance trade, craft monopolies, police, and even a "money-lenders' bazaar". Not money as we understand it yet, but commodity currencies (usually barley and silver), often loaned for as much as 33⅓% per year. The Jubilee or periodic forgiveness of debts (as known in the Bible) already existed in Sumer, which would have otherwise collapsed under the load of debt.

Sooner or later the bank (i.e., the temple) would solve this problem by obtaining the monopoly on money. By lending at interest ten or more times its actual assets, the modern bank simultaneously creates debt and the money to pay debt. *Fiat*, "let it be." But even in Sumer the indebtedness of the king (the state) to the temple (the bank) had already begun.

The problem with commodity currencies is that no one can have a monopoly on cows or wheat. Their materiality limits them. A cow might calve, and barley might grow, but not at rates demanded by usury. Silver doesn't grow at all.

So the next brilliant move, by King Croesus of Lydia, (Asia Minor, seventh century B.C.), was the invention of the coin, a refinement of money just as the Greek alphabet (also seventh century) was a refinement of writing. Originally a temple token or souvenir signifying one's "due portion" of the communal sacrifice, a lump of metal impressed with a royal or temple seal (often a sacrificial animal such as the bull), the coin begins its career with *mana*, something supernatural, something with more (or less) than the weight of the metal. Stage two: coins showing two faces, one with image, the other with writing. You can never see both at once, suggesting the metaphysical slipperiness of the object, but together they constitute a hieroglyph, a word/image expressed in metal as a single meme of value.

Coins might "really" be worth only their weight in metal but the temple says they're worth more, and the king is ready to enforce the decree. The object and its value are separated; the value floats free, the object circulates. Money works the way it works because of an absence not a presence. In fact money largely consists of absent wealth—debt—your debt to the king and temple. Moreover, free of its anchor in the messy materiality of commodity currencies, money can now compound unto eternity, far beyond mere cows and jars of beer, beyond all worldly things, even unto heaven. "Money begets money," Ben Franklin gloated. But money is dead. Coins are inanimate objects. Then money must be the sexuality of the dead.

The whole of Greco-Egypto-Sumerian economics compacts itself neatly into the hieroglyphic text of the Yankee dollar bill, the most popular publication in the history of History. The owl of Athena, one of the earliest coin images, perches microscopically on the face of the bill in the upper left corner of the upper right shield (you'll need a magnifying glass), and the Pyramid of Cheops is topped with the all-seeing Eye of Horus or the panoptical eye of ideology. The Washington family coat of arms (stars and stripes) combined with imperial eagle and fasces of arrows, et cetera; a portrait of Washington as Masonic Grand Master; and even an admission that the bill is nothing but tender for debt, public or private. Since 1971 the bill is not even backed by gold, and thus has become pure textuality.

Hieroglyph as magic focus of desire deflects psyche from object to representation. It enchains imagination and defines consciousness. In this sense money constitutes the great triumph of writing, its proof of magic power. Image wields power over desire but no control. Control is added when the image is semanticized (or alienated) by logos. The *emblem* (picture plus caption) gives desire or emotion an ideological frame and thus directs its force. Hieroglyph equals picture plus word, or picture as word (rebus), hence hieroglyph's power and control over both conscious and unconscious—or in other words, its magic.

We lived in the land of the halter top. We snived in the
snand of the lalter snop. Hip. Pop. Pifflewop.
(Holland, page 69)

From **World on Fire**

Michael Brownstein

PANORAMA OF OIL RIGS, BLEACHED SKY, ENORMOUS WHITE SUN.

Gasoline smell everywhere, you can't avoid it, you can't run inside, there is no inside.

I want to love you, to hold your hand, smell your hair, run my fingers across your brow, lick your skin.

I wish for a lot of things, maybe, but especially these.

Pining for you, unable to sleep in the petrochemical haze, the greasy air, the toxic breeze.

I eat and drink your tantalizing presence nearby, worse in fact than absence.

Because I have you and I don't.

We make love but you're a thousand miles away, your eyes focused on the ceiling.

We make love but you're listening for the phone to ring.

And there is no phone, at least none that works.

It's so preposterous, worse than any joke.

I should have taken it as a warning, I should have known.

I'll never have you to myself.

Your clear glance always denied, averted.

Blood and dust and oil cover everything, the windows, the tables, the chairs.

My lungs—I'm coughing uncontrollably now, my very existence spattered against the grimy panes.

Doubled over, coughing and coughing, stomach sore, I'm frightened, disoriented.

This landscape used to be among the most beautiful on Earth.

Now look at it.

For a moment I can stand up straight again and I breathe deeply.

I look out the window and see huge trucks rumbling by in the sand, each leaking black liquid from behind, trails of crude oil the following trucks slosh through as if during a thunderstorm.

Then—I can hardly believe my eyes—the wells cease pumping, the oil sucked out of the Earth for good, and the endless procession of trucks stops, magically, as if someone's voice which has been calling and calling in vain is suddenly heard.

Will you listen to me? Do you hear me?

Once upon a time—for the longest time, hundreds of thousands of years—the Earth sustained itself.

Forests and meadows and shining lakes.

Herds of animals came and went.

Among them were human beings, communicating in silence with animals, plants, spirits.

Nature was intelligent, it spoke in people's visions and dreams.

Greed—distraction—boredom—cruelty.

You don't believe me when I tell you these things didn't exist then.

Worse than that, you don't care.

It's irrelevant, you say. A fairy tale. A waste of time.

Then why am I chasing you?

Our home is no longer in the great outdoors.

We bivouac in an abandoned cabin, the sagging floors covered with a snowdrift of cold sand, broken tools, shattered glass.

As if everything were inside out, now, once and for all.

I reach out to touch you.

You've aged quickly.

No one would guess this is the same person I followed like someone dying of thirst, up and down busted streets, month after month, and not so long ago, either.

The sun glared at us then.

"I want a new life for us!" I called out.

You kept walking but turned your head to listen to my voice, your hair swinging in the poisoned light, and I was happy.

Now I feel along the cabin walls for the warmth of your face.

Maybe I still need you, maybe I don't.

Whenever we make love now I visualize some unknown wraith from movies or magazines, it's the only way I can get off.

I wonder what will become of us.

Time is not constant, it shakes and folds and twists.

Time is a snake.

The present swallowed by the past.

The future outracing the present.

I hate the way I'm laughed at, ignored, patronized, all because I see the full force of what's coming.

Highways overgrown with trees, oil tankers beached like forgotten toys, the whole petrochemical nightmare vanished.

And in its place?

People are people.

They'll continue to look into each other's eyes and invent the world.

You left me on the morning when the trucks stopped running.

The sky, an eerie lime–magenta mutation, was immense and threatening.

Uncapped fires from the oil wells blazed in the distance.

I gladly would have killed for you, my darling.

To make me forget you, time gave me a small hand mirror in which I look and see nothing, not even the reflection of my face.

Impossible to say who you are now, who I am.

These days the newspapers are full of stories about genetic engineering.

I want to raise my voice.

"Doesn't anyone remember the last mirage we all took for the inalienable truth of our lives? Doesn't anybody have a snapshot of the cars we rode around in? Isn't there even one shred of diary or memoir to bring us back to those times of noise and pollution and disconnect?"

But instead, I have to tell you, I've discovered someone new—
Jesus, she's so lovely she makes my skin crawl.

I'd gladly have a heart attack and die in her arms this very
moment.

She's—but I won't try to describe her.

What could that possibly mean to you?

You who are mesmerized by someone completely different now
too—in fact by the very slob who stands in front of me in line at the
bank, his shoulders slumped, his oily scalp coming apart at the seams
to reveal a tiny frantic brain alive with decay.

Impatient to get to the teller's window and withdraw every last
cent I have in order to blow it on my living dream, for some reason I
turn and look.

There you stand out on the sidewalk, your nose pressed to the
glass, oblivious of everything else, panting for your new beloved.

I wonder if you'll ever even know his name.

In the gathering darkness, none of us able to see.

None of us able to clear our heads and think.

Be still, my heart.

Learn to accept what's coming, sooner than you think.

A new soft-sell eugenics is coming, I'm sorry to say.

People—you'll still call them people.

The question is, what will they call you?

Talk about being shut out.

An ostracism compared to which the school-yard cruelties of ten
thousand years will seem like a loving embrace.

I'm human too. Don't abandon me.

Flaming trees, melting buildings, air as thick as jelly.

Identical blue faces stacked like cordwood.

Waiting to be selected, waiting to be customized, waiting to be of
service.

The custom job of the near future so brilliant as to be unde-
tectable.

Everyone convinced they're rugged individuals.

Living out their lives on a tasty frontier made of digital pixels and
audio.

While further north the polar ice cap has vanished.

In its place palm trees, giant lizards, disabling ennui.

The Inuit wander disconsolate in the heat, unable to perspire, drowning in sights and sounds of a jungle completely alien to them.

Their disorientation blinds them to the tropical beauty surrounding them.

Lost in the impossible made real.

As for me, I take great pleasure in the color photos I've tacked to my cabin wall.

Photos of car bodies, "modern classics" from the fifties, Malibus and Thunderbirds in mint condition but without tires or even wheels, their axles ground into desert sand.

I admit it, I've always wished for the end of our craven, unworkable civilization, no matter what the cost.

Does this make me a monster?

Compared to whom, though?

Compared to corporate vampires sucking blood from the Earth, single-mindedly reducing all difference to sameness?

Or would you compare me to the para-humans, the virtual millions whose time surely is at hand?

Economic globalization, glorious agenda of sameness.

America's gift to the universe.

Victory of death-in-life.

Cloning is the biological version of this sameness.

It won't work without predictability, control, standardization.

Just as globalization won't work without predictability, control, standardization.

Corporations are legally invulnerable and therefore immortal.

They anticipate the soft-sell eugenics to come.

In fact, they bankroll its creation.

Even before it collapsed, our hallucination was in serious trouble.

But we continued living it, that's for sure.

We loved and fought and played.

We scored and were burned.

We hit the jackpot.

We fell on hard times.

Our bright youth faded.

Our hair turned gray, our eyes grew dim.

Terrible new scourges swept through our bodies.

But meanwhile global capital's trance raged on.

To feed its phantoms the non-white world was sucked dry and brought to its knees.

Ecosystems annihilated.

Family lineages morphed into nothing.

Cities metastasized into urban blobs.

People conditioned to disacknowledge the obvious.

In order to understand how this happened, we have to pretend the empire's still alive.

We'll make believe everything's still functioning.

We'll shut our eyes and conjure up Empire triumphant.

We'll pretend the lights are still on, the banks and cafes are still open, the season tickets are still being printed.

We'll have to look at the past as if it's the present.

Not difficult, really.

Since that's the vision which made Empire possible in the first place.

Eaten from inside out, the empty edifice finally crumbles.

But when?

What year is it, anyway?

Centuries ago ancient Mayans predicted world upheaval for the year 2012.

The end of their sacred calendar's five thousand-year Great Cycle.

Has 2012 come and gone?

The future everyone secretly fears, is it already here?

And the past—did it ever really happen?

The high walls of the Incas, the Roman Coliseum, the World Trade Center, all built to last a thousand years—were they nothing more than fever dreams?

When can the monuments of consensus reality be said to exist, no matter how many multitudes have slaved to construct them?

Multitudes in the midst of whose ongoing personal dramas, the actual date remains conjectural.

Since any world described from observation exists relative to the observer.

Perceptions of before and after depending on the perceiver.

Although you're free to watch the evil consummated before your eyes and shudder.

Because now's the time of the motherfuckers.

Whether yesterday, today, or tomorrow.

Whether early or late, inside or out, up or down.

Whether devil or angel.

Which brings us to you, dear reader.

And to me.

The first time I got behind the wheel, what joy! Sixteen years old, a Jewboy trapped in Bible-Belt fifties Tennessee.

What better way to seek release!

I remember my long slender fingers around the red steering wheel.

Red, red, the Malibu inside and out was bloodred.

My foot to the floor, lost in speed, the original disconnect, king of trances.

How many times, slipping and sliding, have I sped around in circles?

Only recently did I make the connection between human blood and gasoline, the blood of the planet.

You could say I'm a vampire too.

I taste your blood when we make love but you can't taste mine, I won't allow it.

Because I'm a vampire with a conscience.

Hepatitis C.

Who knows how or when I contracted it?

Once upon a time I shot speed with a charismatic poet.

I let him talk me into it.

Or perhaps (how I hate irony!) before travelling abroad in the seventies, those gamma-globulin shots for supposed protection against Hepatitis A.

I let the doctors talk me into it.

Is that how I ended up here, by absolving myself of all responsibility?

It's raining now.

The immense desert valley finally softens.

Flames spurting from distant oil wells seem to shrink.

They lose their profligate insistence and appear almost playful, spontaneous, innocent.

Then I notice oil wells by the tens of thousands, spread out across the face of the Earth.

Very few of them are softened by rain.

Because even with the shift of the magnetic poles which occurred in the year 2012, even with the extreme changes in climate we've endured, oil and water still don't mix.

Inside my little cabin, water trickles down the walls and disappears in the sand.

Inside my little cabin, mice chew at the thin lilac cashmere sweater you left behind.

Inside my little cabin, the computer screen glows in the dark.

I can't look at it directly for more than a moment.

My eyes ache, my head swells, my heart—anyway, soon the battery will give out, the screen will go blank.

Then if I want to communicate I'll be forced to rely on telepathy.

What goes around comes around.

Those who came before us communicated telepathically, for tens of thousands of years.

Then, for some unknown reason, people lost the ability to sing invisibly.

And now?

Now we depend on wireless mechanisms beaming microwaves into our skulls.

A few short years from now, brain cancer may be the latest—the last—fashion.

Whoever's left will realize that "information" was a strategy of the transnationals, chaining people to computer terminals for the enrichment of a few.

Their limitless greed.

Their boundless egos.

And whoever's left will finally know what the ancients knew:

Communication is experience, never information.

Communication—whirling dervish of the spirit, red glow of the heart—is never about control.

Emptiness, my great friend.

I was right to have embraced you all these years, while others made their fortunes in oil wells.

Or in trading futures.

Or in some other gleaming facet of the great mirage.

Emptiness, I salute you.

In supermarket lanes and along the crowded concourses of trans-portational endlessness I stand naked before you.

You've kept me young.

My gaze is fresh and eager.

Even in the city, people stop and stare.

Although these days, I don't go to the city much.

Only true diehards remain.

Everyone else—long ago, it feels like, but maybe just yesterday—everyone else jumped ship.

Because the city's the most vulnerable place of all, now that the end times have begun—services crumbled, unclassified diseases sweeping through the populace.

Not to mention the fact that, without trucks or trains or planes, real food is unobtainable.

Everybody's been reduced to eating gummy bears or spoonfuls of their own stinking shit.

Oh, to leave the city behind.

To live quietly and autonomously in the sweet countryside, exist-ing on apples and berries and honey.

Or is this just another dream I had last night?

Last night my little cabin barely survived the wind.

It swept along the desert like a razor, carrying with it smells of burning factories, burning automobiles, burning flesh.

I hid my face in my arms and wept.

Asleep or awake, I listened to the wind.

Fallout from the control culture swirled through my brain.

No fewer than four thousand and possibly as many as ninety thousand species dying out annually.

Tropical forests finished at the rate of one percent a year.

Crop genetic diversity vanishing from the field at the rate of two percent a year.

Irrigated soils eroding thirteen times faster than they could be created.

Fresh water consumption twice that of its annual replenishment.

Two percent of the world's languages extinct every year.

Many of the world's ecosystems occupied by people with no indigenous language capable of describing, using, or conserving the diversity that remained.

Cultural diversity being to the human species what biological diversity was to genetic wealth.

The public at large mystified and silent.

How did the end times come about?

Perhaps a short economics lesson is in order.

We'll shut our eyes and conjure up Empire triumphant.

Please forgive the seeming lack of "poetry" in what follows, dear reader.

Please restrain your impulse to tell me you know it all already.

Open your heart, not your switchblade mind.

Think with the blood which those who came before have bequeathed to you.

I'll pick one corner of the mechanism to describe.

Later you can use your imagination to transfer its workings into other dark corners—

Borrowing countries service their international debts by increasing their borrowing.

The more they borrow, the more they depend on borrowing, and the more their attention is focused not on development but on obtaining more loans.

Exactly like heroin.

Exactly like the systems crash that diabetics experience.

Integrating domestic economies into the global economy means removing import barriers.

This virus undermines the integrity—the self-definition—of nations.

Increasing the export of natural resources and agricultural commodities drives down prices of export goods in international markets—creating pressure to extract and export even more, simply to maintain earnings.

The very process of borrowing creates indebtedness that gives the World Bank and the IMF power to dictate policy to these nations, whose leaders, in order to stay in power, can only become more and more corrupt.

Diabolique

Foreign loans enable those governments that have bought into the process to increase expenditures without the need to raise taxes— always popular with wealthy decision makers.

This artificial jolt—does it remind you of cocaine, a thousand times more potent than the coca leaf?

Does it remind you of amphetamine?

Does it remind you of petrochemical fertilizers, driving plants to a frenzy of artificially induced growth?

Parallels everywhere—economic, environmental, psychological, physical.

Drug addiction equals petrochemical addiction equals global capital's addiction.

Nothing is arbitrary, nothing occurs in isolation. Nothing is left to chance.

Returning to the matter at hand—

Those officials who sign foreign loan agreements tie their people to obligations outside public review or consent.

This becomes especially outrageous when the projects displace the poor, pollute their waters, cut down their forests, and destroy their fisheries.

Then, when the bill comes due, social services and wages are cut to repay the loans.

The bottom line, the arithmetic of need: too much foreign funding prevents real development and breaks down the capability of a people to sustain themselves.

The system works to increase production of more things that people who are already well-off want to buy.

Luxury items for the first world.

Poor people seldom buy imported goods.

Their needs are met by simple locally produced goods.

From the standpoint of transnational corporate capital, people-centered development is a major problem.

It creates little demand for imports.

It creates little demand for foreign loans.

It favors local ownership of assets.

Whereas the "structural adjustment" policy of the World Bank means building dependence on imported technology and experts. It means encouraging consumer lifestyles, displacing domestic products with imports, driving millions of people from lands and waters on which they depend for their livelihood.

It means recolonization of poor countries by transnational capital.

It means hidden subsidies for petroleum and transport so food from the other side of the planet costs less than local.

It means replacing intrinsic value with utility value.

Diabolique

This arrangement brought darkness to the world, while the sons and daughters of its perpetrators played in DVD fields of fantasyland.

Did these children have any inkling of what their lives cost others?

Let's take a real-time example. In Haiti—

"Agribusiness receives ample funding but no resources are made available for peasant agriculture and handicrafts, which provide the income of the overwhelming majority of the population. Foreign-owned assembly plants that employ workers (mostly women) at well below subsistence pay under horrendous working conditions benefit from cheap electricity. But for the Haitian poor—the general population—there can be no subsidies for electricity, fuel, water, or food;

these are prohibited by IMF rules on the grounds that they constitute 'price control.' Before the reforms were instituted, local rice production supplied virtually all domestic needs. Thanks to one-sided 'liberalization' it now provides only fifty percent, with predictable effects on the economy. Haiti must 'reform,' eliminating tariffs in accord with the stern principles of economic science—which by some miracle of logic exempted U.S. agribusiness. The natural consequences are understood: a 1995 USAID report observed that the 'export-driven trade and investment policy' will 'relentlessly squeeze the domestic rice farmer,' who will be forced to turn to the more rational pursuit of agroexport for the benefit of U.S. investors. By such methods, the most impoverished country in the hemisphere has been turned into a leading purchaser of U.S.-produced rice, enriching publicly subsidized U.S. enterprises."

(*Profits Over People*, Noam Chomsky)

But what about the science behind agribusiness?

Surely its goal is the welfare of humanity.

Genetically engineered "golden rice" and "golden mustard oil" heralded as miracle cures for vitamin A deficiency, from which millions of children suffer.

Who would reject such a gift?

But look closer, dear reader.

Follow Monsanto's presence in India—

The stage was set by the Green Revolution of decades past.

Instead of millions of farmers breeding thousands of crop varieties to adapt to diverse ecosystems, the Green Revolution reduced agriculture to a few varieties of a few crops.

At the same time, herbicide manufacturers bought up seed companies in order to develop plants that liked their product.

This led to genetic erosion as well as large-scale pollution from agrichemicals.

Mustard greens rich in vitamin A traditionally were eaten by India's rural poor until mustard cultivation was wiped out by monoculture of wheat and one-dimensional breeding of mustard for oil, destroying the edible nature of the plant's leafy part.

Monsanto described its involvement as philanthropic, but breeding was covered by patents making its rice and mustard the company's exclusive property.

Then, under "free trade" policies, mustard oil was banned in 1998 to allow unrestricted imports of U.S. soy oil. Imported oil now accounts for fifty percent of India's consumption.

The dumping of oil from Monsanto's genetically engineered soy displacing whatever mustard cultivation remains in India.

And vitamin A deficiency becomes a problem Monsanto offers to solve.

(From "Blind Technology," Vandana Shiva, *Bija Newsletter*)

But how does this lead to the end times, you ask.

How does it relate to drinking the last drop of gasoline?

To an uncontrollable invasion of genetically modified virus?

To losing track of what human means?

Start with the fact that I take advantage of you but I'll never trust you.

You're an eternal threat to me because to enrich myself I have to I exploit you.

I put myself in your shoes and feel your resentment.

I build engines of destruction to defend myself against you.

But then I realize it's far better to co-opt you instead.

So I use mass media to neutralize you even before you become a threat.

I'm trading in futures of fear, dear reader.

I'm projecting my model of the aggressor in every direction.

I don't let up until your uniqueness has been enveloped in my profit machinery.

Until you've been educated to serve me.

Better yet, to join my corporate fantasy which stretches across the seas and around the globe.

In my corporate fantasy everyone sees what I see.

Everyone wants what I want, thinks what I think, eats what I eat.

Everyone enriches my already obscene fortune, enriches it without end.

Everyone serves my insatiable need for more. Peoples of the wide green Earth, suck my devious white asshole until the end of time.

When is a motherfucker not a motherfucker?

When he's not aware of the consequences of his actions?

But ignorance of the law is no excuse.

Drill her in the heart with your machinery and she'll return the favor with sickness and plague.

Desecrate her fields and she'll suffocate you with pestilence.

Force cannibalism on her cattle and she'll eat holes in your brain.

Ignore her and she'll rob you of your contentment.

Embrace a culture of sameness and she'll hold up a mirror.

And wherever you look, no matter how fast you turn your head, the mirror will remain front and center.

What will you see?

You'll see one size fits all.

You'll see yourself lose your balance.

Once you start falling, how will you stop?

Are you afraid to look in the mirror and find no one there?

Do you scramble to reconstitute the someone who went to bed the night before, ego intact—heck, forget the ego, what about your face?

What about your distinctive body odor, your hard-won achievements, your head stuffed with memories?

You look in the mirror this morning and suddenly nothing's there, although miraculously your usual vantage point remains the same.

The same windows behind you, the same greenery outside.

Yet you're invisible, transparent.

Without baggage, without memories, without a body, even.

And outside those windows behind you, summertime oak trees sigh in the humid wind.

Above them, a prehistoric sky, more green than blue, with clouds so majestic they silence your muttering mind.

How many millions of years have passed and the sky's remained the same?

Before you came here.

Long after you've gone.

History a scrim laid over another order of time—vast, luxuriant, spacious.

History an invention—an insertion—making us believe the only time is clock time.

Clock time doing to original time what enclosure did to the commons, what monoculture does to the forest.

Paradise not a place but a kind of time.

Time in which we once roamed, unbounded and unhurried.

Animals in the wild never hurrying except in crisis. Unlike our everyday mode of stress, burnout, hormonal loss.

We all sense the cramped artifice, the acceleration.

Everyone knows what's going on but no one will say it.

Chasing the bus of the rest of our lives.

Genuflecting to Our Lady of Perpetual Crisis.

Get two hundred anytime minutes, plus one thousand night and weekend minutes.

A realm of straight lines, of superimposed agendas.

(The first act of the Chinese invaders, upon conquering Tibet's wide-open plateau, was to assemble forced-labor gangs as an introduction to the State's discipline. These gangs built stone walls in the middle of nowhere, straight lines leading to nothing.)

But the unbounded time of those who came before has never deserted us.

It is primal, everpresent.

It is oceanic, omnidirectional.

Time of the plant realm, almost inconceivably slow for us now.

Almost inaccessible without the aid of an ally. Without meditation, vision quest, fasting, psychoactive substances.

Something to help break the trance.

I cut the star-shaped cactus into slices and cover the slices with water, simmering them for hours.

During this process their wrenching smell pervades the cabin.

That indescribable aroma.

Its singularity makes me know I'm in the presence of a formidable plant spirit.

Simply cooking the cactus brings that spirit near. Someone calling from just beyond the threshold of hearing.

Something appearing just beyond the threshold of sight.

Heal me, momma. Heal me of this disconnect.

I get more and more nervous as the afternoon proceeds.

Many trips to the bathroom. Butterflies in my gut, sweat on my brow.

Anticipation of the psychoactive powerhouse to come. San Pedro will blow my ego apart, it will leave my identity in tatters.

Glory of the unknown.

Emptiness, my great friend.

An afternoon of preparation has come down to this: half a cup of pale brown liquid which I raise to my lips and drink.

The taste is beyond bitter, impossible to gag down, but I do.

Half an hour passes and my body starts to feel inhabited, tentative.

As if the atmospheric pressure in the entire universe dips and changes.

Suddenly fear gives way to anticipation, acceptance.

I look to rejoin the ancient ones, those who came before.

I look to leave the toxic comic book of consensus reality far behind, my taste for the infinite quenched again at last.

Maybe this time, spirit, you'll answer my question.

Teach me how to survive the collapse which surrounds me in every direction, on every level, at every step.

Make me strong enough to dismantle the demon.

Heal me, momma. Blow me away.

And spirit tells me this—
"To dismantle the demon, you have to turn and face him.
Because the demon eats your nonawareness.
He drinks your complacency.
Either you turn and face him or he's on your back forever."

Not only face the demon but swallow him whole.
But eating poison's impossible without guidance.
To teachers both human and plant spirit I offer my gratitude.
Their shower of blessings protects and instructs me.

Their gift to me, mind's empty nature.
Their gift to me, fearless presence in the midst of conflagration.
And the demon's solidity becomes my creation.
Evil loses its power, despair no longer seduces.
Faced with the end times I'm renewed, energized.
Empowered by realizations I'd never have otherwise.
I experience hell realms without hesitation.
No more exciting time to be alive than now.

So don't lose heart, dear reader.

Take courage as we enter the dead zone, where planetary decimation is disguised as unprecedented material well-being.

We'll watch, disbelieving, while millions of people are given mysterious new identities.

We'll listen to canned music distract drunken revellers in surfside vacation colonies, while those locals not employed as security stare open-mouthed from the other side of barbed-wire fences.

None of this registering in suburbs back home, where overfed families bicker like strangers, then line up at the multiplex to watch glacial rituals of dismemberment and sexual predation.

We'll swallow all this and more, remaining self-possessed, remaining present, until gradually the demon will shrink, like a tumor in spontaneous remission.

And the space for a new life will appear.

New York City: Street Photographs Following the Terrorist Attack on the World Trade Center, September 2001

Ken Schles

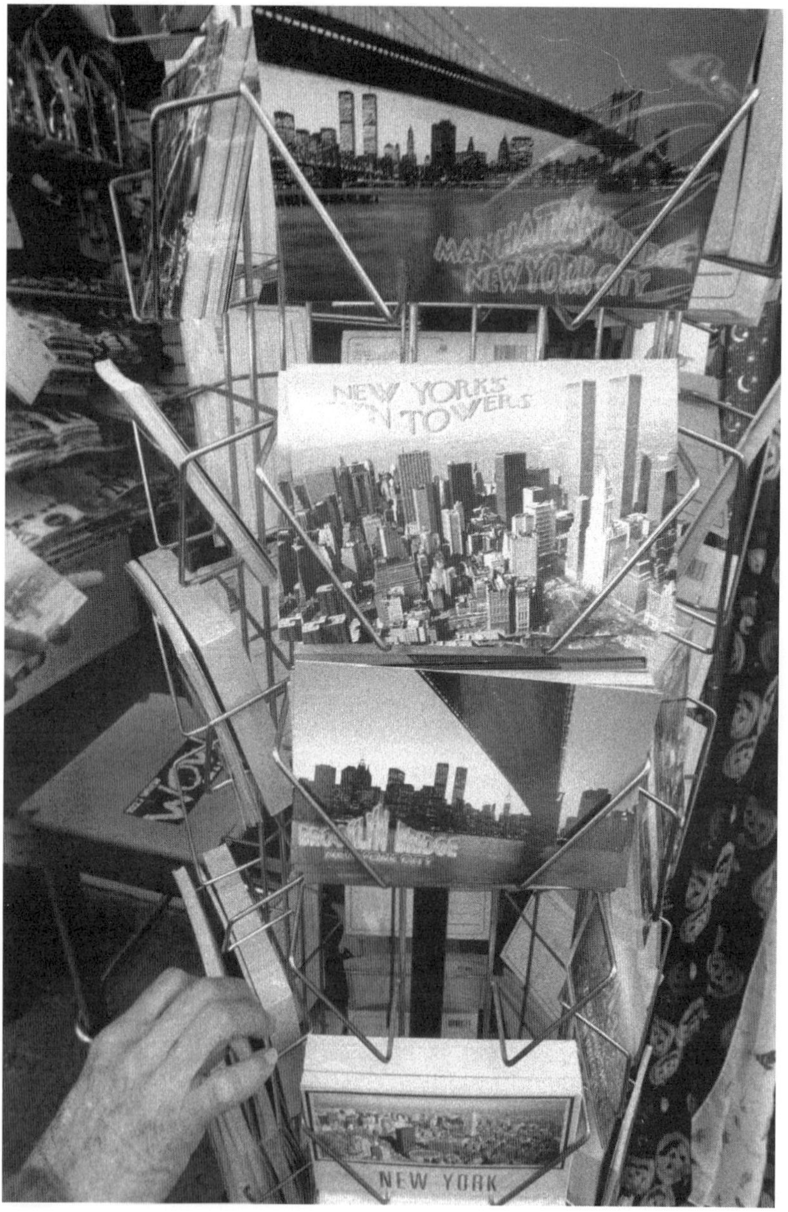

NEW YORK'S
NEW YORK

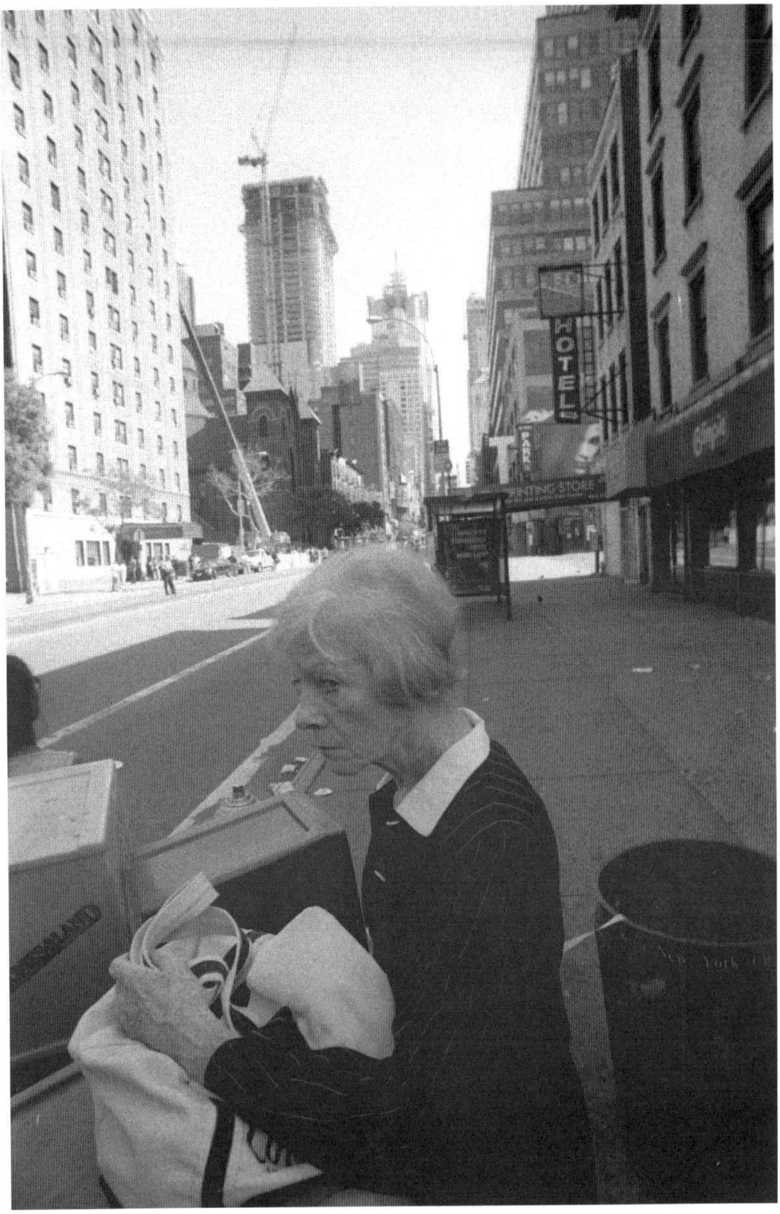
HOTEL

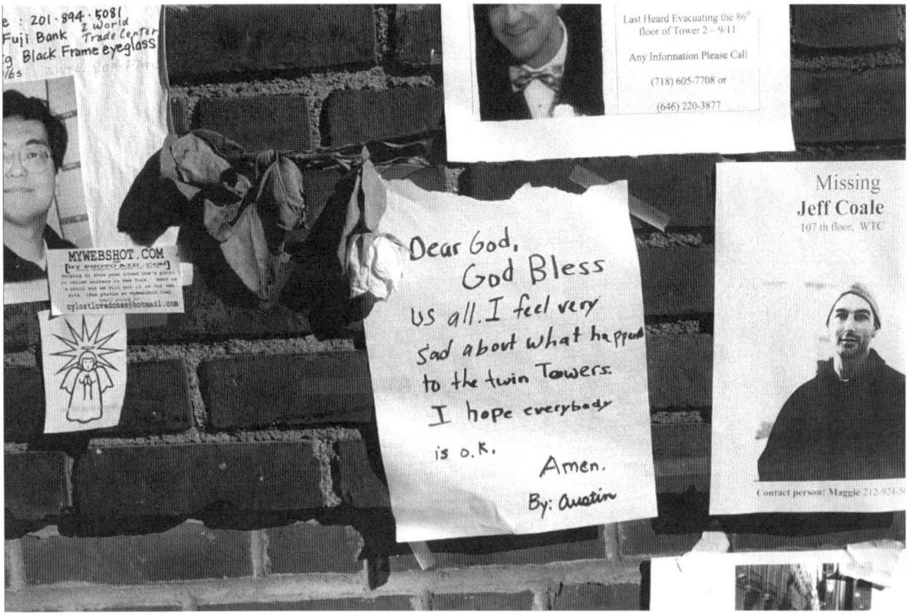
201 · 894 · 5081
2 World Trade Center
Fuji Bank
Black Frame eyeglass
MYWEBSHOT.COM
Last Heard Evacuating the 86th floor of Tower 2 – 9/11
Any Information Please Call
(718) 605-7708 or
(646) 220-3877
Dear God, God Bless us all. I feel very sad about what happ
to the twin Towers. I hope everybody is o.k.
Amen.
By: Austin
Missing
Jeff Coale
107 th floor, WTC
Contact person: Maggie

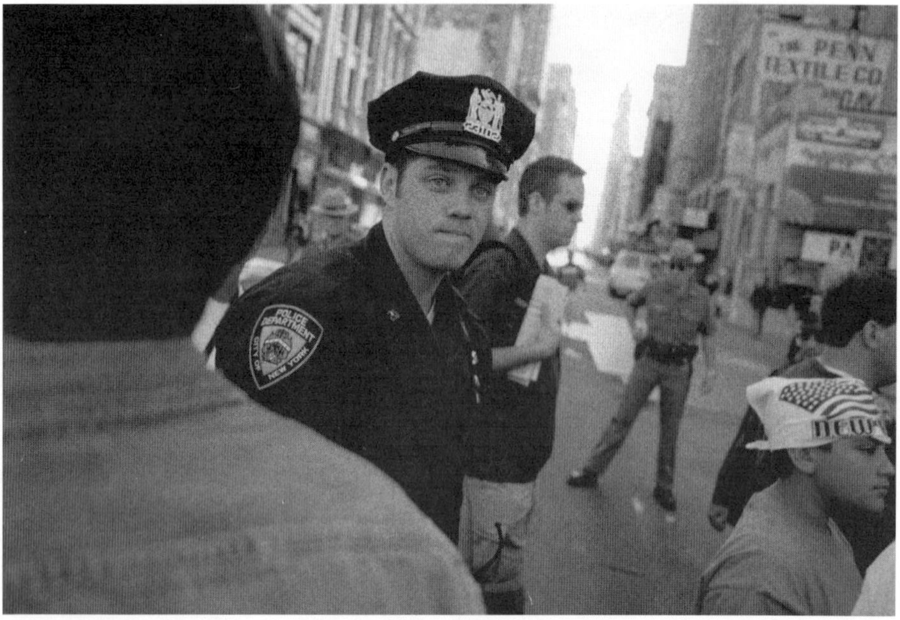
PENN
TEXTILE CO.
POLICE DEPARTMENT
CITY OF NEW YORK

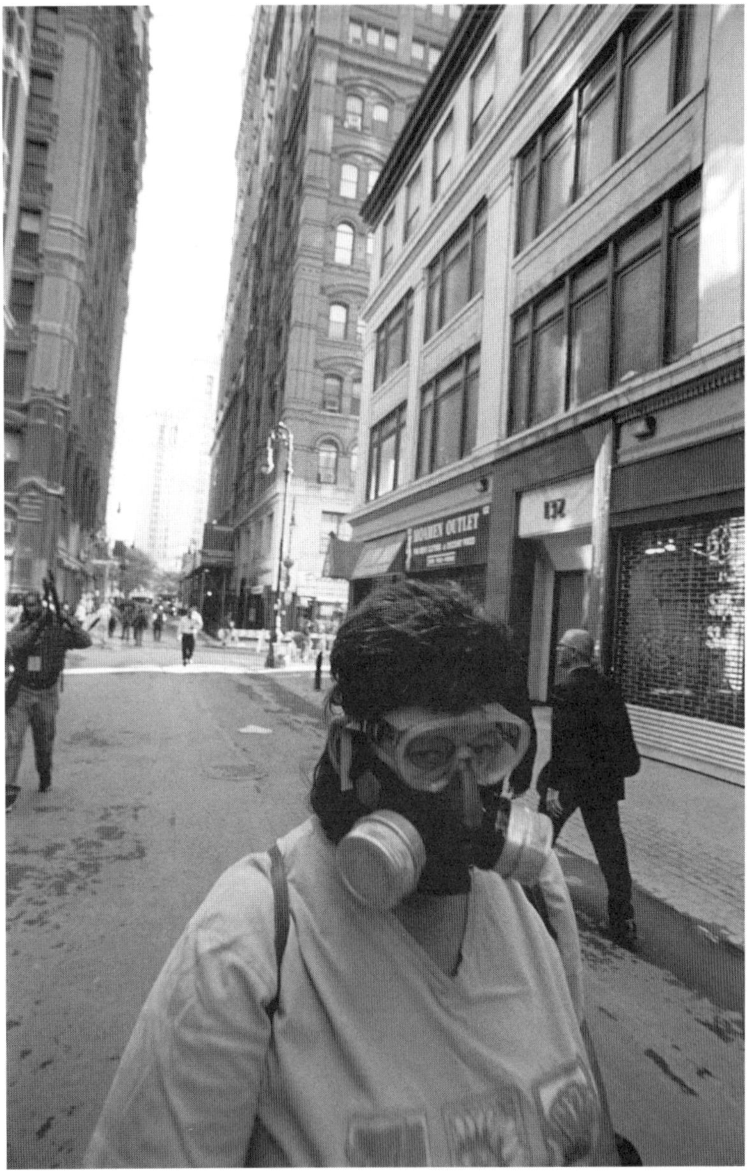
OUTLET

LETTERS

Significants You May Have Missed

I am very glad you folks are alive and doing what you're doing. If only *Open City* had more money to do more of that. I'm sorry I don't have any to give you either. Alas, these are my tiny suggestions.

1) I would like to see more promises in the form of promiscuity. Take, for instance, the now well-documented fact that Sèvres porcelain teacups from the era of the French Revolution were not modeled on Marie Antoinette's breasts, and that Christ's eye color was not blue but a rich chocolate brown. Or, something more nowadays: in thirty-seven percent of Americans, the thirst mechanism is so weak that it is often mistaken for hunger. These may seem like insignificant items, but if your desire is to reach the widest possible audience, not everybody mind you, but wide, I suggest that you, as editors, establish a section detailing "Significants You May Have Missed." It's just a thought.

2) I would like to see more aesthetic judgments bantered about. Where a cocktail party probably succeeds when the small size of the room relates inversely to the number of people it contains, there's no room for mediocrity. Even if it is easy and reliable and, well, often olympian. I am not suggesting intolerance, though I must add that tolerance is an euphemism for self-segregation; I am suggesting appreciation, but only for those things truly liked. Unless one is quite honest in one's likes and dislikes. It is not enough, either, to publish what you like—you must point out what you don't like. You only live once, some say, so if you don't like the blue color of my shirt or the blue of your blouse, please point this out.

3) I would like to see an essay on the currency of nepotism. If you cannot find someone who you don't know to write it, I shall volunteer.

Now that it's dark, my dear friends, please feel free to say what you like.

Mark Yakich
Tallahassee, Florida

We Didn't Write This

I am sorry that you have received no letters. It is wrong, and I know how you must feel. There was a time when I was a letters page editor. I didn't want the job when I was assigned it, and I wasn't very good at it, but still a kind of odd pleasure accompanied the few fine letters we got and those I published. Even so, I believed this job was beneath me, and before I would do what it was I did, I tried to explain this fact to the magazine's owner. But the job was mine and I was the job's, and so I was forced on.

Every other Friday the letters went to the art department and into pages, and so Thursday night I would compose twelve to twenty letters. It was fun for a few issues and then it became unpleasant and quickly I began farming out much of the work. A fact checker, a copy editor, an editor from a sibling magazine, my unemployed friend, Chad—for more than a year they supplied me with the letters. Some were handwritten, some typed, all had envelopes with postmarks and return addresses, which I needlessly stapled to the letter for an added element of authenticity, before delivering the small pile to a fact checker—not the one who wrote the letters—and throwing a bigger real pile into the trash.

Okay, so why would you want to know this? Perhaps you suspect my writing to be motivated by the special prize: this is not the case (though (1) I am curious if there really is a special prize and (2) what it is). The reason I am writing: if you continue forward with your letters page, but you continue not to get any letters, and there's all that white space, do you think I could have it, kind of become the Letters Page Adjunct Curator? I have the above mentioned experience, I am good on deadlines, courteous, professional, have good references, and don't expect any remuneration other than the pride of making something good.

Please advise soonest.

Albert Music